EVOLUTION OF A MONSTER

by

J Steffy

A HellBound Books Publishing LLC Book
Houston TX

**A HellBound Books LLC
Publication**

Copyright © 2018 by HellBound Books Publishing LLC
All Rights Reserved

Cover and art design by J. Steffy for
HellBound Books Publishing LLC

No part of this book may be reproduced, stored in a retrieval system, or transmitted by any means, electronic, mechanical, photocopying, recording or otherwise without written permission from the author This book is a work of fiction. Names, characters, places and incidents are entirely fictitious or are used fictitiously and any resemblance to actual persons, living or dead, events or locales is purely coincidental.

www.hellboundbookspublishing.com

Printed in the United States of America

Dedications

Becky for walking me through the submission process and allowing me to bounce ideas off her during the writing process.

Also, to all the murderers that let me pick their brain when I was a prison guard; they provided much inspiration for writing.

Evolution of a Monster wasn't written just for a read, it was written as a follow-along experience. Though the names, houses, and addresses are all make-believe, the streets, roads, cities, and landscape are all real.   When read, while referring to a map, Evolution of a Monster takes you on the killer's journey for real. You can find the streets on a map, and see his actual path through woods, rivers and towns; and it is especially fun for those people who live on the actual streets, and who have been through these towns...

EVOLUTION
OF A
MONSTER

March 1, 2014 (9:15 p.m.)   Somerset, KY

Stepfather (1)

Dear Diary, you have been created to track my bucket list adventure. I have made it my mission to kill at least 50 people in 50 states before I depart from this planet myself. But first, I should introduce myself. My name is Vance Estep and I live in Somerset, Kentucky, about a mile from Lake Cumberland. I'm 25 years old, about 6 foot tall and 211 pounds. I wish I could say it was all muscle but alas I cannot. I also reside with my mother and two younger brothers.

Since my early childhood, I have felt different than everyone else. I was never what one would consider an outcast but I have always experienced difficulty relating to the emotions of others. Though I may never truly understand sadness, regret or fear, I have educated myself on the appropriate physical responses in many emotional situations. For instance, the death of my stepfather brought great sadness to everyone involved with the funeral proceedings, but all I could think about was how crooked his tie was. I understood that I needed to blend in, so I just looked toward the ground with my forehead in my palms for about two minutes, and then I looked up, frowned a little, then looked back to the ground. I repeated this pattern until I was allowed to leave. Several people patted me on the back and said "*Sorry for your loss*" as if they were somehow responsible. No one appeared to have an inclination that his life was ended by my hands.

I have always had a constant desire for something unknown. Growing up, I could never figure out what it was. The sensation seems to originate in my stomach and spiral its way throughout the rest of my body. I assumed it had to be some kind of sexual urge that had gone unsatisfied for too long. Over time, I have tried every sexual fantasy I could imagine, while attempting to satisfy this beast that lives inside of me. Nothing has ever worked, and I contemplated suicide on more than one occasion. The feeling is unbearable, and there seemed to be no other way out.

On January 4, about two months ago, I had finally decided to end it all, and I was ready for it to be over. It was about midnight and everyone in the house was in bed. I crept quietly toward the kitchen, trying to avoid the squeaky spots on the floor. I had removed a large stainless steel steak knife from the silverware drawer and sat down at the kitchen table to cut my wrists. I had no concern with the bloody mess I would create, since I would not be around to clean it up. I knew I should have been saddened by the thought of my mom walking in and having to clean up after me, but I wasn't. As I held the blade to my wrist, I became entranced by the reflection of the moonlight on the blade. At that moment my hairless little stepfather walked in and witnessed my actions. His endeavor to stop my plan developed into a silent struggle, which resulted in the knife being accidentally inserted into his throat. My hand was on the handle when it happened and my face was near his. I felt the vibration as the knife disconnected his jugular. I felt the warmth of his blood running down my wrist and I watched as the life left his eyes.

I felt reborn that night. It was the first time I have experienced internal peace of that magnitude. The beast was gone and I felt like a real person. For a brief instant, I could even sense a form of sadness while I stared at him lying lifeless on the gray, blood soaked tile. The sadness quickly faded but my life-long, unexplainable desire had finally been satisfied. Nothing in my existence had even come close to the euphoria of that moment. I wiped my prints from the knife and opened the kitchen window, hoping that his death would be treated as a robbery gone wrong. I don't know why I was even concerned about my prints because I've never had them scanned into a database before, but it's better to be safe than sorry. Before returning to bed, I stared out the window for a couple minutes while washing my hands and trying to make sense of my feelings. The moonlight glistening on the snow-covered hillside brought me even more peace. I watched my breath in the winter air and attempted to make smoke rings. I didn't want that night to end, but I couldn't be caught standing by a dead body.

I awoke that morning to my mother screaming and I was not a suspect. I struggled for three days as the wonderful feeling began to fade and the beast returned. As excruciatingly uncomfortable as my life was prior to his death, it had become even worse. Now that my urge was identified, I realized I had some decisions to make.

It was already clear that I would rather die than to live in agony. I understood murder was wrong, and if I were captured, I would be sent to prison. After some deliberation, I determined I would submit to my cravings and live the rest of my days in peace. I decided to never see the inside of a courtroom.

I will make the police kill me instead.

March 6, 2014 (7:20 a.m.)   Somerset, KY

N/A

Dear Diary, today is the day I set off on my journey. The anticipation has been building and I cannot procrastinate any longer. My reason for killing 50 random people is simply because I cannot rationalize killing for another reason besides self-satisfaction. I have tried to find a particular group of people to target for moral purposes, much like that Dexter guy from the television series. However, I don't really see anything morally wrong with merely selecting random people once the decision to murder has been made. Besides, it would be too much work to study people before killing them. I'm not trying to make a statement or play God with people's lives; I just need to quench my thirst. 50 is just a goal, if I have a chance to increase my tally, I will. The purpose of canvasing all 50 states is because I have always wanted to travel and this seems like the perfect opportunity. The 24-hour period following the passing of my stepfather was the high point of my life. It had to be comparable to someone discovering heroin for the first time. It took about three days for me to come completely down from my high, so I don't want to wait any longer than that between my kills.

This goal is not accomplishable if I remain in one location. I should be able to move from one capital to another without being spotted, as long as I stay on the road. My only concern is trying to get to Hawaii and Alaska without my trail being discovered. Perhaps I will save them for last, since I will be prepared to take my own life after I'm done anyway. However, if I really think about it, there's no way I'll get that far. How smug would I have to be to think my goal is accomplishable? I'm going to try though.

March 6, 2014 (10:15 p.m.)   Harrodsburg, KY

Benjamin Whales (2)

Dear Diary, according to my directions, I live only one hour and forty-nine minutes from Frankfort Kentucky - taking 27 North to 127 North. Since it is the closest capital, it makes sense to travel there first. I left home with nothing but a back pack full of essentials, you, and a newly sharpened ten inch fillet knife. I also had to tell my mom and brothers that I had joined the army and they are shipping me to Afghanistan. I still had yet to determine my means of transportation. I decided to walk until I figured it out. Remember, I'm not exactly a professional at this.

Luckily for me, Benjamin Whales was passing through on his way home to Harrodsburg and figured I needed a ride. He said he could get me that far and I told him it was better than nothing. He was driving a rusty red, single-cab pickup truck. He looked about thirty years old with a thick face of hair. His taste in music was slightly bizarre based upon his appearance. He seemed to be a metal head but had bluegrass tuned into his stereo.

Once we reached the stopping point for my ride with Benjamin, I pointed out an old buffet on the corner of James Trail. It was a little brick building that had to be a hundred years old, and its slightly hidden parking lot was perfect for my next step. It was 6:30 p.m. and the only car on the property had a for sale sign, so I assumed the place was vacant. He pulled in with the intention of dropping me off and going back home to watch a movie with his family. It didn't take long for him to realize my plans were a bit different than his own. Idling near the corner of the restaurant, I quickly scanned the area for potential witnesses. Benjamin attempted to shake my hand but unfortunately for him it was reciprocated with a knife through the belly button. It was obvious that I underestimated his will to live once he grabbed my throat with both hands, attempting to strangle me. I'm only thankful that I jammed the knife with the blade facing up because as I reacted to the choking, I pulled up on the knife and it sliced him open all the way to his rib cage. I had no idea how easily human skin was to cut. It's curious that we can withstand some of the abuse we put our bodies through. He was very surprised when he looked down to see all of his intestines spilling out as if they were being dumped from a five gallon bucket. It was like he just realized that he'd left the oven on at home or something. I got to watch as the life shimmered away from his eyes. That seemed to be one of the main variables to my ultimate satisfaction.

I thought having blood run down my wrist was exhilarating, but it was nothing compared to having it cover my entire lap. The beast was vanquished once more and I sat in that parking lot for 45 minutes with my body completely limp and at peace with the world. I felt like I had just had the best sex humanly possible. All of my concerns and troubles faded away. Once the blood began to coagulate and the body resting on my shoulder began to chill, the realization of what I had done started to sink in. I had to leave before being spotted. I may not be able to understand regret, but I do know that I don't want to get caught this early in my journey.

March 7, 2014 (11:45 p.m.)   Frankfort, KY

Phil Turner (3)

Dear Diary, once I arrived in Frankfort yesterday, I spent the rest of the night looking for a place to hide the truck and body. After some exploring, I found a boat ramp to the Kentucky River right off of Lawrenceburg Road. I believed I could push the truck into the marina and it would sink. Prior to pushing the truck into the river I searched for anything useful. He had a wallet with $120 in his pocket. He also had a handgun with a full clip in his dashboard. I had to use a change of clothes from my bag. It became quickly apparent that I did not pack enough clothes for the trip. I found a large flat rock on the bank of the river, lifted it, and stuffed my soiled clothes underneath. I set the truck to neutral and pushed it down the ramp. Once it hit the water, it just sat there, taunting me. I had to continue pushing it until I was in the water up to my hips before the current finally took over. I don't know if the river was shallow or if the truck was floating but it bobbed along the surface as it traveled downstream.

I know someone will discover the evidence soon, if they haven't already. I'm not planning for an extended stay here, so I'm not overly concerned. I hiked through the woods until I encountered a street named Meadow Lane. I needed a place to sleep for the night and I didn't feel the urge to kill anyone else, so I decided to remain unnoticed. I found a house with an unlocked detached garage, containing a silver speed boat with a red racing stripe. I slept in the gray carpeted floor of the boat with river drenched clothes for the night. It wasn't very comfortable and I believe I was stabbed by a hook once or twice, but it was much better than sitting at home, hiding from myself.

I don't remember what time I finally dozed off, but I was awoken at 7:30 a.m. this morning by the boat owner screaming at me. He was wearing a green robe and flip flops and was holding a wireless house phone. As he yelled, I couldn't escape the pungent odor of coffee and cigarettes. He was convinced that I was a homeless man squatting on his property. He threatened to inform the police if I didn't leave his boat immediately. I still didn't feel the urge to kill, and I won't just do it for fun, so I apologized and departed from his garage. I have never been an angry person and I typically do not get upset due to the actions or behaviors of others. I am astonished however, that people are capable of reaching that level of emotion. Though I respected his right to live, I still don't think he deserved it.

Since I was still feeling good, I decided to spend the day touring the countryside. While walking along the river skipping rocks, I began to realize I haven't eaten or showered for several days; I hadn't eaten since breakfast on the 5th and my last shower had been roughly two days prior to that. I had the money I received from Benjamin, so I decided to book a hotel for the night. I walked for about an hour before finding a Hotel on 127. Upon inquiring about the price of a room, I realized that I had to walk away if I wanted to have money for food. I don't understand how people are so willing to spend that much money just to sleep on a bed in front of a television. The uncomfortable feeling began sinking back in as I searched for some kind of fast food. I then decided to just take someone's house for the night - and possibly take their life in the process. Besides, the last guy hadn't even been in the capital. But why am I hung up on the whole capital thing anyway? As long as I'm killing someone somewhere in the state, I'm still accomplishing my goal.

I' m actually sitting in bathtub feeling like a new man as I write this. You have to hear how I got here, Diary.

I think I am starting to discover my niche. I carefully selected the perfect house at the edge of a tree line on Murrell Street. I picked this house because it had one old beat up car, an unmaintained yard, and no sign of resident children. I knew I would be killing whoever lived in the house, so I was hoping for an older couple without kids. I figured an older couple would be easier to take down, and if there were kids involved, I'd probably kill myself before harming them. I'm just fulfilling my destiny, I'm not some kind of animal. When I finally get caught, I'm not going down as a child murderer.

I don't remember the time, but the sun had fallen to meet the horizon. As I approached the front porch I could hear yelling and crashing within the small brick house. I stood by the front door grasping my knife and scoping for witnesses. Due to the high level of commotion inside the house, I began to second-guess my initial judgment. Just as I decided to walk away, the front door opened abruptly. Standing there was a very angry man about two inches taller than me and much skinnier. He was wearing nothing but red boxers - thick hair covered his torso, reminding me of a caveman. I couldn't tell if he was trying to grow a beard or was just too lazy to shave. Before I could say anything, he grabbed me by my shirt and pulled me through the threshold of his house. The front entry was basically a small dim-lit hallway.

He yelled into the living room, which was around the corner about ten feet away from where we stood, "Is this the fat bitch you're fucking?!" I quickly thrust the blade into his ear until the handle contacted his lobe. He released my shirt in a panic and began stumbling in the opposite direction, down the front hall, passed the living room and toward the kitchen. I ran after him and tackled his legs. I then pulled out the knife and began stabbing him in the back until he stopped moving. I could actually hear air escaping his lungs through the holes in his back and it reminded me of the leak in my air mattress at home. It's obvious that my knife is too narrow because people are taking too long to die. If I was a hunter, I don't think anyone would buy my videos. I think I'm trying a different method from here on. Plus, it is getting boring already. The killing still brings me satisfaction, but I'm starting to think that it should be a little fun as well. If this is something that I have to do to stay sane, I might as well try to enjoy it more.

I suddenly remembered that another person was in the house, so I ran into the living room with the intention of making tonight a two for one. Balled up in a corner was a cute young girl about my age –or maybe a little younger – with long brown hair soaked in tears and blood. Her bottom lip was busted and her left eye was nearly swelled shut. She was crying and begging for me to spare her life. Looking at her, I had no intention of hurting her any further. I'm not sure if it was compassion or lust, because I'm pretty new to both, but I definitely started to feel *something*. I asked her if anyone else was in the house and she informed me there was a baby up stairs. Suddenly, something happened inside my body that I was unfamiliar with. My heart began to pound and my face started to get very hot, so I told her to remain seated and I returned to the body in the hall. I rolled him over and proceeded to punch him in the face until the feeling left my body. Afterward, I was left with my desired state of calm while admiring his shredded profile. Mangling his face was somehow more fulfilling than the knife. I don't know where the anger came from, but it felt amazing. For a moment, I lost contact with the rational part of my consciousness and began to act on impulse.

I had a conversation with the girl to determine my next move. When she realized I wasn't planning to kill her, she began to express her appreciation for saving her. She explained how she would have been dead by the end of the night if I hadn't arrived on time. She told me his name was Phil Turner and she has been trying to leave him for a couple months, but he wouldn't allow her. We agreed that I will spend the night and make myself at home. When the morning comes I will tie her feet up and leave through the back door. She will give me a couple hours before calling the police. Her story will be that someone in a mask came in and started yelling at her boyfriend. He killed Phil, beat her, and then left. The time span will be explained in that her hands were tied up and it took that long to get them free. I'm going to leave the knife in Phil because it's useless and the link between it and river boy will make her story more believable. Okay, she just walked in and is sitting on the toilet, smiling at me.

March 8, 2014 (9:05 p.m.)   Indianapolis, IN

Ted & Teresa Fuller (5)

Dear Diary, I left through the woods this morning. Perhaps one day I'll return and check in on her. I'm not sure how she washed the blood out of my clothes but I'm glad I didn't have to lose two outfits in one night. I believe the police may have sighted the truck that night because I heard several sirens while I tried to sleep. I knew that law enforcement would be informed about Phil's murder soon, so I searched for transportation out of town. I pondered on riding a bus, but I remembered they were equipped with cameras and I couldn't risk exposure. As I strolled through the housing projects of

Oaklawn Drive, I noticed a thick built woman in her 40s wearing a white striped business suit, walking toward her silver SUV; I decided I would ask politely for a ride to Indianapolis.

I approached the driver's side from the rear as she opened her door. I said, "Excuse me, May I get a ride?" She jumped at the unexpected sight of a male figure approaching her. She rudely told me that she didn't have time for bums and to step away from her car before she called for her husband. I put the tip of Benjamin's gun against her stomach and calmly said, "Try again, Zebra." She agreed to take me wherever I needed to go as long as I didn't hurt her. I climbed into the passenger side and concealed the gun under my shirt. I demanded her phone and she began crying, as if I were stealing her virginity. Once she reluctantly handed it over, I turned it off, and then tossed it in her shrubs before we left the driveway.

While passing over the river on 127, the police and news crews were as thick as mosquitos. There was very little discussion during our trip besides the exchanging of names. She identified herself as Rose Miller, a local bank manager. She just kept whimpering and praying. It's rather humorous that just an hour earlier she was so cocky and rude. Shortly after crossing into Louisville Kentucky, a news bulletin aired on the radio. It chattered about the details of Benjamin and how he was from Harrodsburg but found in Frankfort. They also talked about a possible connection to the death of Phil. I could see the panic wash over her face as she realized who she was riding with. We had just traveled through a tunnel on 65 approaching the Mellwoood Avenue exit when she decided to leap out of the car like a frog on crack. I guess she believed her odds of living were better by jumping out of a moving vehicle going 60 mph.

I seized the steering wheel to avoid a collision while I observed her body splatter on the road and get flattened by a school bus following behind us. It was like nothing I've ever seen in movies. She didn't roll into the grass or even remain in one piece. She pretty much exploded on impact and the bus just smeared the pieces along the road when the breaks were engaged. I climbed into the driver's seat and continued toward Indianapolis. I didn't kill her, she did it herself, so I'm not counting it. I knew that it wouldn't be long until the police identified her and the vehicle I was driving. I didn't have time to waste looking for another car, so I took my chances and drove straight through. I spent nearly two hours on the road thinking I would be caught at any moment.

I came to a residential area called New York Street and parked in front of someone's garage. It was 5:32 p.m. and the uncomfortable feeling started to spiral throughout my body. At that point, I wasn't concerned with profiling the house. The only prerequisite I was searching for was a garage in which I could hide Rose's SUV. The moment I parked, a man in his 30's approached to ask if I was lost. He was about 5' 9" with a buzz cut; he was dressed in a football jersey and sweats. He was of a stocky build and seemed like he might have been a jock in high school. I was concerned that there were children inside, but I had no other options. I told him my car was overheating and I just need somewhere to park it for about 20 minutes. I apologized and stated that I would be out of his driveway once it cooled. I've learned that apologizing to someone when there is no reason to apologize induces an instant sense of trust.

As I had anticipated; he accepted my story and invited me to accompany him on his porch for the duration. His name was Ted Fuller and he was, unsurprisingly, a high school gym teacher. He had a wife named Teresa and two daughters, ages three and eight. We talked for about 25 minutes and the topic of the "Kentucky Killer" came up more than once. I thanked them and said I had to be leaving, but asked if I could use their bathroom first. Ted invited me into his house and guided me up a flight of stairs to their bathroom. I walked in and contemplated my next move. All I had was the gun, and it would be too loud. Additionally, I knew that if I attempted to strike him with the stock of the gun, he would likely remain unscathed and commence to beating me into a pulp.

I rummaged through their cabinets looking for a silent and effective weapon. I had made it this far and I wasn't about to risk being seen in that SUV any longer. I was reluctant because I didn't know what to do about the kids. The older one could identify me but I wasn't about to hurt her. I decided to just take care of the parents and then I'd figure out what to do with kids later. I found a large pair scissors, clogged the toilet with a rag, and then yelled for Ted once the water started to run out onto the floor. He rushed in, grabbed the plunger and started plunging away. The wife and kids were not in sight so I jammed the scissors into the back of his head just above the neck. Based on experience, I imagined he wouldn't die easily, so in the same instant, I swept his legs and shoved his face into the toilet using the scissors as a handle.

Once he stopped squirming, I removed the weapon and proceeded into the hall to yell for Teresa. I announced that Ted needed her help. I stood at the top of the steps as she approached with her girls following eagerly behind her. I had my fingers through the scissor handles with the blades aiming outward. I couldn't help but to giggle when I recognized my uncanny resemblance to Wolverine from *X-Men*. She approached me at the landing and I punched her in the eye, piercing the back of her skull with the tip of the scissors. I know how hard a skull can be, so I was surprised by my own strength - I must have been in character, LOL. She died instantly and the kids began screaming. I couldn't let them attract the attention of neighbors so I aimed the gun at them and told them to shut up or die. I directed them into the hall closet and put a chair against the knob so they wouldn't escape while I moved the SUV into their garage.

March 9, 2014 (8:50 a.m.)   Indianapolis, IN

N/A

Dear Diary, this morning I still wasn't sure what to do about the girls. I have tried to cheer them up and even put in a movie for them to watch while I cooked their dinner. I thought *The Little Mermaid* could cheer up any kid. I recognize they are sad about their loss, but I'm sure they'll get over it. After watching over them throughout the night, I have to be the closest thing to a parent they have now. Both girls have blond hair and resemble their mother more than their father. Amber is three with blue eyes and multi-colored fingernails. Heather is eight with brown eyes and was dressed in a princess role-playing outfit. Amber is not very articulate, so I'm not concerned with leaving her as a witness. I will abandon her when I leave and someone should find her before she goes hungry. I will take everything out of the cabinets and leave it on the floor for her. Heather, on the other hand could easily identify me so I have decided to allow her to accompany me on my journey rather than taking her life. She may come in useful later on when I'm trying to gain someone's trust.

I took Heather to the bathroom to mask her identity before we departed and she became hysteric at the sight of her parents still lying where they dropped. It had been over 24 hours since their death and she was still freaking out about it. I couldn't have someone with me who was going to scream at the sight of blood. I understood some training was in order so I sat her beside her mom and handed her a kitchen knife. I explained that she needed to merely push the knife in half way and I would reward her with a cookie. She attempted to refuse so I grasped her hand to assist her with the task. Once the blade was in the throat of the body, I could see her begin to loosen up. I had her repeat the action five more times on her own, and then another five on the father's body. By the time that exercise was complete and she received her cookies, she was ready to leave with me.

The best way I could think to disguise her was to convert her into a boy. I gave her a short, spiked haircut and kept all of the hair trimmings in my bag so no one would know of her transformation. I found the most gender neutral clothes she possessed and asked her change into them. It was a pair of loose fitting jeans and a white t-shirt. Her shoes looked fine except for a pink stripe going down the side. I colored it in with a black permanent marker. Now she looked and sounded like an eight year old boy. I took the same marker and pushed some ink into a saucer of water to make home-made hair dye. I used a toothbrush to darken her eyebrows. Now, her brown eyes made more sense with dark eyebrows. She was surprisingly excited about her new appearance as we agreed on her new name being changed to Zachary.

March 10, 2014 (9:10 p.m.)   Columbus, OH

Old Woman (6)

Dear Diary, we made it to Columbus, Ohio around 12:00 a.m. today. I haven't slept yet but Zach slept the whole way cuddled up in the back seat with the body of the vehicle's owner. It was kind of cute how he reminded me of a big kitten. I'm proud of how well he is adjusting to his new lifestyle. He didn't cry or scream while I commandeered the vehicle from an old woman sitting at a traffic light. On the radio, they were still talking about the "Kentucky Killer." I don't think they have found the people in Indianapolis yet or they would have realized the link and stopped labeling me with that silly little nickname. "Kentucky Killer"; what kind of name is that anyway? Can they not think of anything more original? Listening to the news stories made me feel amazing. It's ironic that I'm finally being recognized for something but I cannot take credit for it. From the sound of it, they have no idea that I'm even traveling.

Zach had been through a lot in the past few days so I decided to treat him to a day of fun. I had just killed yesterday and I don't plan to do it again until I need to. I want to have as much of a father-son bonding time possible. I hid the wrinkly old body in the trunk and took Zach to *Chuck-E-Cheese*. I spent almost $100 on pizza and games. I think we'll be okay on money for a while now because I collected $800 from Ted's drawer, $50 from Phil's wallet and $210 from the old woman's purse. Not to mention the $120 I still had from Benjamin. So far, I have made $1180 on my expedition and I haven't even had to pay for gas. Nor have I had to pay for food, since I can fill my bag with munchies at every house I visit.

Zach excitedly pulled me from game to game, having the time of his life. We had a pizza eating contest and everyone standing around us looked at us like we were crazy. His laughter made me feel compassion toward another person for the first time. I realized today that I would never let anything happen to him and I began second guessing my whole mission. It's like a light just came on or something. I've never seen a human before that I could actually feel seeing me back.

March 11, 2014 (11:55 p.m.)   Columbus, OH

Donald & Allison Shaw (8)

Dear Diary, even though I had no urge to kill last night, I had to in order for Zach to have a safe place to sleep. I can't expect him to sleep in a garage or something. I'm responsible for another person now and I have to act more responsible. We couldn't have just stayed in the car because I knew people were probably looking for the old woman. There was a used car lot on Sullivant Avenue, which was closed for the night but had no gate to prevent us from driving straight in. We left the vehicle in an empty parking spot in an attempt to camouflage it with the sales inventory. We walked along Sullivant until we arrived at a house with no signs of children. I still do not wish to harm a child but I cannot adopt any more, either.

We came upon a small, 2-story house with light blue shingles and a ridiculous amount of yard ornaments. Since I didn't feel the aching desire to commit an unnecessary murder, we set at the corner of the back yard discussing methods of a quick attack. Zach appeared to be a little nervous and was insisting that we just get a hotel and leave the people in the house alone. I had to explain to him that I could not use my ID - for tracking reasons. After some deliberation, I was able to convince him that we needed this house for adequate shelter. We just needed to determine how to do it. Zach spotted a 10 pound sledgehammer leaning against the back door.

With the hammer in hand, I stood by the back door so I wouldn't be spotted by someone peering out the window. I told him to knock on the door then back up to the steps to lure the person onto the porch. He did as I asked and we stood in our positions until the homeowner turned on the porch light. After seeing a little boy on his porch with a book bag, he opened the door quickly and asked if Zach was ok. As soon as the man was clear of his doorway I swung the hammer like a baseball bat with every ounce of my strength. I succeeded in connecting with his chin and it folded his head inward toward the hammer. I expected his head to fly off or at least bounce off the hammer but it actually engulfed the iron sledge and pulled it from my hands as he toppled backward. The sound of the wooden handle hitting the screen door while he lay there convulsing woke his wife. I heard her call out for *Donald* so I rushed toward the kitchen entryway and waited for her.

As soon as she noticed him on the ground surrounded in a pond of blood, looking like he was trying to eat the hammer, she attempted to scream. I jumped behind her from my hiding spot and grabbed her mouth to keep her quiet. I tried to snap her neck like I was in a ninja movie, but it was very difficult. Every time I twisted her head, her body would just twist too. I decided I would try to choke her with my other arm that was already around her neck. During my struggle with the slightly overweight middle-aged woman, she suddenly stopped protesting and fell to her knees. I became aware that Zach was standing in front of me with his hands over his mouth in astonishment. Before I could ask him what was wrong, I noticed a steak knife sticking out of the woman's chest. Apparently Zach will come in more useful than I initially foresaw. Later, I found some mail that revealed the woman's name as Allison Shaw. It took a while to decide if I was going to count Zach's kill in my total but since he's my kid, I'm responsible for what he does, so I'll count it.

March 12, 2014 (9:00 p.m.)   Columbus, Ohio

N/A

Dear Diary, last night Zach came in and slept beside me. He was afraid to sleep in the living room so close to the bodies. He said they might wake up and get him. I explained the impossibility of his fears in an attempt to help him rationalize. It actually made me feel really good that he felt safe with me. I still can't explain the sensation I experienced when he took down Allison. It had to be similar to what a dad feels when his child accomplishes bike riding without training wheels. Ending someone's life myself helps to alleviate most of my stress and anxiety but watching him do it warmed my heart.

Though I was very proud of him for stepping up to the plate like that, I experienced mixed emotions as I drifted to sleep. He was sleeping so peacefully and I didn't want the night to end. I wished I didn't have to do the things I do. I wished we could just move to a suburb somewhere, enroll him in school, and lead normal lives. My life was finally starting to become so simple before he walked into it. I was just going to keep killing until I killed myself. I have faced my own fate and have decided that this is the path for me, but seeing his innocence fading made me feel like shit. I don't know if that is what regret feels like, but if so, I don't like it at all.

While I sat around the house today trying to decide what to do next, Zach came to me with a grin on his face and a hand full of boy clothes about his size. It appears that these people were grandparents. It was a relief to know I could avoid going into stores a while longer. As he took a bath, I browsed the channels trying to find a comedy to start our day with an upbeat vibe. I stopped on a news report that was covering the "Kentucky Killer." They also found Amber but there has not been a link between the murders yet. Investigators must have not searched the garage. Police also put out a missing child alert for Heather, so I need to avoid watching the news in front of her.

We decided to stay another night in this house, since there were no visitors and I've been feeling better than ever. I had to drag Donald into the kitchen and wash the back porch to avoid detection from neighbors. We shut all of the blinds in the house and locked the doors. I've learned that Zach has a very good imagination and enjoys pretending he's an astronaut or a princess. He included me in all of his hallucinogenic adventures and I gladly participated. Having prolonged exposure to some dead bodies has helped him cope tremendously. By lunch time, he had begun stepping over Allison to enter the kitchen without hesitation. I just hope that he will not be scarred by my actions. I understand that this must be difficult for a person of such a tender age.

March 13, 2014 (7:05 p.m.)   Columbus, Ohio

N/A

Dear Diary, I'm being blinded by the beast today. I have tried to ignore my urges but they are beginning to prevail once more. Having Zach in my live has caused me to reconsider my mission. He has shown me how to feel compassion and regret. If something bad would happen to him, I'm sure I'd experience sadness as well. I've considered remaining in this house until I'm captured, and then Zach could be taken to a stable home. However, I also believe that continuing my journey and bringing him along for the ride is the only real option. I know he would be happier with me than in the custody of foster parents.

March 15, 2014 (2:45 a.m.)   Rockwood, MI

Officer King & Random Man (10)

Dear Diary, I realized Zach's true potential last night and I am no longer reluctant to move forward with my plans. Around 9:00 p.m. we were relaxing on the couch watching cartoons when he asked me if we were going to send anyone else to heaven. He had created his personal reality, entertaining the belief that I was an angel of God sent to deliver people from their physical existence and that he was destined to assist me. I initially thought he was going crazy, but I later began to wonder if his beliefs could be substantiated. It made sense to me because there should be no other reason for me to have this strong desire to commit murder. I've never really hated anyone and I had a pretty decent childhood by my mother. I mean, I got picked on in school, but nothing that would have made me into the person I have become. There has to be some kind of explanation for why I am who I am. Why else would a person be hard-wired to feel peace only when ending someone's life? Also, how is it possible that I could randomly stumble across Zach, who is the only person who has succeeded in making me experience real emotions? Perhaps this is all for a greater purpose. Although I'm not a religious person, I cannot rule out some kind of spiritual intervention, because my actions were unexplainable until this point. If I'm not preordained for this life, I'm sure God will find a way to tell me.

I revealed my intentions to Zach, and he seemed excited to be a part of it. He said he would enjoy going to different states. He also loves the idea of never going back to school. Talking with him about everything was surreal. He did not judge me and he was so eager to hear all of the details. I informed him that I was trying to quit because he deserves a normal life and I would like to be his new father. He hugged me and said "Thank you, Dad, but we have to keep going." I was amazed by his level of maturity and his willingness to accept me as his dad. I was overrun with happiness, but I still couldn't suppress my increasingly unbearable urge to feel the warmth of blood between my fingers. It was decided that we would gather supplies and continue our journey together.

We rummaged through the house, searching for anything useful before we departed. I found $310 in a purse that was sitting on the coffee table. Zach found a five inch hunting knife that hooked to his belt loop. Only moments before departure, we heard a knock on the front door. I didn't know what to do, so I handed my gun to Zach and told him to only use it if in case of an emergency. I looked out the peep hole and saw a police officer, who announced himself as Officer King. He said that Donald's employer informed the police of his unusual absence and he's been sent to check on him.

I opened the door and introduced myself as Max Shaw, a nephew to Donald. I explained to him that my uncle was bedridden with an illness and could not be disturbed. He asked to come in and verify. I knew I had to cooperate or he would call for backup. I allowed him in, realizing that he would notice the bodies on his way to the bedroom. At that moment I had accepted my fate of being arrested and Zach not being allowed near me. I didn't desire a shootout because I didn't want him to witness my death. I just dropped my head and told him to come on in.

He walked past me and came to Zach, who was standing about six steps behind me. The officer stopped to inquire about his wellbeing. Zach looked like he was about to cry and he pointed to me saying I hit him. I was appalled because murder was something I was ready to face, but not abuse. King turned quickly to detain me and I watched his eyes disappear as a bullet traveled up the back of his neck and through his eye sockets. My ears were ringing and I was covered in bloody debris. I was stunned when the officer dropped to the floor, and I noticed Zach standing across from me holding my gun, smiling from ear to ear. I confiscated the gun, quickly grabbed everything we were taking and ran to the minivan in the driveway. During the evacuation of the house, I lectured Zach about making good decisions. I told him that he couldn't just shoot someone without us having a prior discussion. He was apologizing and I could see that the fear started to come back to him again. I had to stop beside the van to tell him that I would have rather gone to prison than to have a cop's blood on his hands, but I was proud of him for taking command of the situation.

We had to switch vehicles before the police began searching for it. We drove down a street called Hague Avenue and began looking for a car. A black SUV with tinted windows was sitting idle at a stop sign and I hit the bumper just hard enough to gain the driver's attention. When he got out to investigate for damages, Zach and I got out too. When the man reached the back of his vehicle, I pulled out the gun and demanded he climb into the back of his SUV. He did so without hesitation and Zach climbed into the back seat. I ran to the driver's seat and we began our trip to Michigan. While I was cleaning my face and trying to change my shirt, the man was sitting in the trunk area behind the back seat yelling at me to get out of his vehicle and to leave him alone. He was making too many demands for someone who knew we ad a gun.

The SUV appeared to be a recent purchase, with leather interior and an amazing stereo system. The owner was wearing a blue dress shirt and a red tie. He had short black hair with gray highlights. He began gaining more confidence, and yelled louder with each new demand. I assumed he was some form of business leader who was accustomed to ordering people around and degrading them. I was content with all of the screaming, until he directed his attention toward Zach. I tuned everything else out, but as soon as I heard, "And look at this little bastard!" I was done with him. I pulled the gun from the band of my pants and handed it to Zach. I continued driving as I looked through the rearview mirror to witness Zach turn around, rise to his knees and fire two shots into the man's chest. My boy calmly turned back around, handed me the gun, buckled his seatbelt, and drifted off to sleep. I need to find more .45mm bullets because I'm now down to only twelve and we have much land to cover.

We drove 75 North most of the way here. We were heading toward Detroit, but by the time we arrived here in Rockwood, I was too tired to continue driving. We stopped at a 24 hour Wal-Mart to sleep in the parking lot. Zach is laying down in the back seat now. He must have unbuckled his seatbelt at some point during the trip to become more comfortable. I still can't get over how peaceful he looks when he is sleeping. I have sat here for the past hour watching people walk in and out of the store, all with no concerns, appearing completely happy with their existence. I wish I could feel like that for more than a couple days at a time. Zach had surprised me today when he jumped into action like a full grown adult, but those deaths didn't provide me with much relief. I just want to push the gas and run over as many people as possible. I can't escape my urges. Perhaps I can be satisfied by cutting a body that is already deceased.

March 15, 2014 (4:30 a.m.)   Rockwood, MI

N/A

Dear Diary, I'm prepared for sleep now, but I had to share what it was like to take my time with a body. I climbed over my son to reach the man who was balled up in the back corner. I reached back over the seat to gently remove Zach's knife from his hip. I didn't want to disturb him because he'd had a pretty eventful evening as it is. I felt a wave of excitement wash over my body as I rolled the man onto his back. The anticipation alone began to alleviate my pain. I observed the accuracy of Zach's bullet holes, wondering how he even knew how to shoot a gun. The thought never crossed my mind prior to that moment but it's obvious to me now that her first father must have trained her.

I started by removing all of my clothes because I didn't want to get more blood on them. I decided to sharpen his right pointing finger like a bone pencil. The blood was cold yet satisfying. As I peeled away at his knuckle, I was reminded of a time in my childhood in which my mother was teaching me how to peel a potato. She kept saying, "Now be careful, because you don't want to cut your finger." I didn't realize how hard it was to remove a person's rib but I was finally able to get the bottom two. My plan was to put holes in the top of his head and insert the ribs to make him look like he had horns. However, I was unable to quietly break through the skull so I just stuck them through his nose holes to give him tusks instead. The amount of exertion required left me exhausted. My urges have faded for now but not to the extent I'm now accustomed to.

March 15, 2014 (9:55 p.m.)   Detroit, MI

N/A

Dear Diary, we finally arrived in Detroit around 2:00 p.m. I still felt a bit unfulfilled, but at least I made it through the day without killing anyone. We spent some quality time together touring the town, with no intent to remain hidden. We went to a Museum and some kind of artistic street project. Zach liked the museum but he really enjoyed the street art. All of the houses and cars were transformed into artistic statements. All I could think about is how stoned the creators must have been to nail stuffed animals all over an abandoned house. From the look of it, I believe it may be the perfect place to release some frustration later. There are plenty of places to hide and the majority of the houses in the area appear to be vacant.

I purchased a newspaper in a gas station because I noticed that Heather and I had made the front page. They have finally connected Kentucky to Indiana but Ohio hasn't been linked yet. It seems I'm staying one state ahead of the police. According to the news story, my name has been changed to "*The Traveler.*" It seems more fitting but I'm just relieved they have no suspects yet. Police have been dragging rivers and searching fields for Heather, hoping to find her body. Everyone is assuming that she's already dead. I tried to hide the article from Zach but he saw the picture of his past self. I thought he would revert back to the sobbing little girl I initially met, but to my surprise, all he said was, "Look how hideous my hair was." Speaking of hair, his eyebrows are starting to go blond again, and it wouldn't hurt to darken the hair on his head as well.

While living life as a real family for once, I have decided to stop hiding from society. We earn money at every stop but I've been cautiously avoiding stores. We were successful in getting a hotel room by the river tonight without using an ID. They attempted to reject us, but I turned and told Zach we'll have to sleep in the car because I'd lost my ID. The front desk clerk told me she would make an exception and allow me to pay with cash if I included the cost of the deposit. We were both very excited when we entered our room. Zach wanted to go swimming but we didn't have clothes for him to swim in. We went to a store down the street and picked up some hair die, swimming shorts, snack food, Vodka, and a couple toys he just had to have. I'm fine with him playing with dolls because he really is still a little girl at heart. The cashier was so forcefully polite that I wanted to slice off her fake freckled little smile. I could tell that she believes I'm a bad parent for purchasing alcohol in front of my son.

When we arrived back at the hotel we changed into our shorts. Zach displayed some concern that his bathing suit did not include a top. I told him he's a boy now so no one cares if he doesn't have a shirt. I haven't had a drink for several weeks so I wanted to get a little buzz before going to the pool. Zach was standing at the door eager to go but he agreed to postpone a little longer if I shared my drink with him. I thought it might be immoral but I figured if he was old enough to shoot a cop, he's old enough to have a drink. I mixed the Vodka with Sprite and we sat there drinking until we couldn't stop laughing at each other. I actually had to carry him to the pool because he was too unstable on his feet and I didn't want people to know he was intoxicated. Maybe I could have played it off like he was just being goofy but it wasn't worth the risk.

At the pool, Zach saw a woman floating on her back and whispered in my ear, "We should go over there and hold her under the water." I told him that it sounded fun but we would surely be caught doing something like that in public. I spent most of my time there trying to teach him to swim. I showed him doggy paddle but he sank like a rock every time I let him go. He invented a game that I accompanied him on. We would go into the sauna, get really hot, then run out and jump immediately into the pool. It was a body shock that I will never forget. After arriving back to the room we ordered pizza and ate in the middle of his bed, watching black and white westerns. Later, I dyed his eyebrows and hair brown.

This is how life should be. I don't think I've ever had a more terrific time with someone. I have suppressed my urges all day and I think that I can avoid killing anyone else as long as I can stay busy and entertained. I'm not a suspect and Heather is assumed dead. If we quit now, we could live a normal family life together and we could frequently have wonderful days like this. I now have a reason to live and since my journey ends with death by police fire, I would like to stop while I'm ahead.

March 16, 2014 (9:25 a.m.)   Detroit, MI

Jay Michaels, his mother, his friend (13)

Dear Diary, I woke up this morning around 3:00 a.m. with a very nervous, tingling sensation spreading throughout my body. I felt like I was going to explode if I didn't do something to release the tension immediately. I looked over toward Zach's bed and he was sleeping serenely as always. I didn't want him to wake up while I was gone so I woke him to ask if he wanted to come with me to the abandoned house place, or stay in the room. He grasped my arm and said he never wants me to leave him alone. With that, we made our way to our vehicle equipped only with my gun and his knife.

On our way to our destination, the odor of the body had become so pungent that it attracted Zach's attention. I heard him say, "What is in his nose?" I told him that it was his ribs and they were supposed to be tusks like on an elephant. He began to laugh uncontrollably, leading me to believe he still had some alcohol in his system. We parked along Preston Street and made our way through all of the artistically positioned debris. Based on the appearance of the neighborhood, I assumed there would be someone walking around late at night, and I was correct. While we crouched down near a bushy fence attempting to remain unnoticed, I observed two men lightly arguing while they walked down the sidewalk. They sounded like they could have been thugs, but I knew that even a thug would try to help a lost child.

I asked for Zach's knife and directed him to run toward a dilapidated house across the street, calling for his mother. He did as I asked and I stayed in the bushes. He caught the eyes of the two men, who then began to approach him while I quietly trailed behind. When the men were closing in on Zach, he walked into a large hole that was in the side wall of the house. The hole was only big enough for one person at a time. I remained low to the ground trying to plan my next move. They appeared to have a short discussion as one man performed a quick security scan, and then crawled through the hole while the other waited outside. By this time I was at the corner of the house. As soon as the first man was completely out of sight, I crept up behind the second man and stabbed him in the side of the throat hoping to sever his trachea and reduce his ability to vocalize his distress. It didn't take but a couple seconds for him to die silently.

Feeling reinvigorated, I crawled through the hole and listened for the location of the second man. I heard some struggling in the next room so I bolted in as fast as I could. He had Zach pinned to the floor holding his mouth shut, attempting to unzip his own pants. I didn't want to kill this guy, because I knew that Zach needed to be the one to do it after what he was attempting to do. I pointed the gun at him and said, "Freeze, it's the police!" The man put his hands up, believing I was an officer. I introduced myself as Officer King and told him he was under arrest; to not move or I would blow him away. Zach came to me and wrapped his hands around my waist. I asked the man his name, where he lived, and who else would be in his house. His name was Jay Michaels, he lived a block away, and his mom was the only other one in the home.

I really wanted to do something special with Jay but the abandoned house wouldn't be good enough. I told him that we would walk to his house and he could pack a change of clothes to take to jail with him. We exited the front door so he wouldn't discover his friend's body. He was sobbing like a little baby the whole trip, trying to explain how what I saw wasn't accurate and how he can't go to jail because he's all his mom has left. He said it would kill her and I told him it probably already has. He didn't know what to make of my comment but he continued toward his house. He asked me why I wasn't dressed like a cop and I told him that I was off duty, on my way home when I noticed that he followed a child into an abandoned house. Zach held my hand the whole way and he kept gripping it tighter every time Jay spoke. He knew what we were going to do when we arrived at Jay's house so he remained calm and silent the whole trip.

When we arrived at Jay's house, we followed him through his front door and his mom was waiting up for him. She was an older woman, about 75 years old, sitting in a recliner watching a game show, surrounded by a thick cloud of cigarette smoke. She screamed when she saw someone was holding a gun to her son. Jay was sobbing, asking for her forgiveness and that he was going to jail. As this went on, I handed the knife back to Zach and said, "Take her quickly." I then told Jay to drop to his knees and put his hands behind his head. He complied and he got to witness as Zach ran from behind, jumped on his mother's half-reclined torso and commenced to stabbing her as quickly as his little arms could go. The woman tried to struggle but her first wound was in the mouth and every time she tried to block the knife, her arms were slashed. He kept going even after the woman was dead. I actually had to call him off.

Throughout the whole incident, Jay was screaming for Zach to stop but I told him if he moved, he would eat a bullet. By the end, he was on his knees with his face to the floor calling for his mama. He said, "You're not the police!" I replied, "That's right, I'm the father." I asked if he had a basement but he wouldn't reply to me anymore. Zach found the basement door and I had to kick Jay in the ribs a couple times to motivate him to move. Once we reached the steps I kicked him in the back, forcing him to tumble down the steps and get knocked out. I was worried at first, because I thought I was the one who'd killed him. After checking Jay's vitals, I was relieved to find a strong pulse. I stretched him out, face up on the steps and with some wire I found, tied his feet tightly to the bottom step and hands to the highest step he could reach.

Zach and I discussed what he would do to Jay after he woke up, and I was amazed by his level of creativity and anger. He asked me to remove all of the man's clothes, so I cut them off and stepped back to watch the show. He rummaged for tools while Jay slept. When the man woke, the volume of his screams made me regret keeping his mouth free. I had to wrap duct tape around his head a couple times to muffle his voice before allowing Zach to begin. I was feeling great after I'd cut the other guys throat, but this was an added bonus. My urge to kill was gone, but I was still excited to see what Zach was going to do. I wonder how much *normal* people would pay to see this.

The first thing he grabbed was a carpet staple gun and he began stapling Jay all over his body. Zach did this until there were no more staples, and he brought the gun to me, his big puppy dog eyes, asking me to reload it for him. Afterward, he emptied it again, climbing the steps to reach higher locations. When this phase of Zach's project was complete, Jay was squirming around, trying to scream, covered in a red glaze where all of the little blood draws ran together. Unfortunately for the man, his scrotum was resting perfectly on the edge of a step and his penis was stapled to his leg. Zach reached down and grabbed a hammer and began pounding away on those gross little testicles of Jay's. After about the twentieth hit, they were no longer attached to his body. I believe Jay had reached a high level of shock, because he was shaking and his eyes were rolled toward the back of his head. Zach dropped the hammer and returned to my side. We stood there for about fifteen minutes, watching as Jay's life ended painfully slow.

I can't explain how peaceful I felt at that moment. My body had no weight, and I forgot about all of my worldly concerns. We stood there as father and son, completely fulfilled. My urges had gone after I killed Jay's friend, but anger had arisen when I saw Zach as a victim. Watching Zach work on Jay was almost as satisfying as doing it myself. It had to be due to how enthusiastic he was about it. That must be how it feels to other people when their kid begins excelling in a sport. I was proud of him, but also concerned that he'd almost gotten hurt.

When we arrived back at the hotel, Zach was already asleep, so I carried him to the room and placed him in his bed. I can't sleep, but I'm going to let the boy sleep as long as he needs, even if I have to pay for another night. After everything he'd just been through, he deserves a good rest. I feel like a normal person once more. My mind isn't clouded and I can think clearly. I'm just soaking in this great feeling of relief. However, I don't wish to continue this, because we will eventually be caught and will have no chance for a great life. I have noticed that as my urges grow stronger, I begin to rationalize more and think less. It's like I'm a completely different person until the deed is done and I return to my relaxed and centered self. Killing 50 people in 50 states is just stupid; there's no way I'll be able to accomplish that goal even if I wanted to.

March 17, 2014 (9:35 a.m.)   Lawndale, IL

Teen Boy & Girl, Woman & Son (16)

Dear Diary, Zach woke up before we had to check out, so we decided to leave. Our room was in good condition, so we received our deposit back. We're on our way to Springfield, Illinois, but we had to make a pit stop in East Chicago so we could exchange vehicles. The SUV guy has to be on the missing person's list by now. I thought I could just do the same bumper technique again for another car exchange, but the people around Chicago are nuts. We drove around until we came up behind a smaller, blue sports car sitting at a stop sign. I hit the rear bumper just enough to get the driver's attention, but instead of getting out to look at the damages, a boy no older than nineteen, and his girlfriend got out and started screaming at us. They didn't care if the collision was an accident, or that I had a kid with me, they just wanted to attack me for hurting their car.

We were on a residential street, so I could have taken one of them, but if the other had screamed, I'd be spotted. I backed up and showed my middle finger to them, hoping that their anger would cause them to follow me. They trailed behind me until we reached a gravel road off of Calumet Avenue. As soon as we were better hidden, I stopped the car and waited for them to approach. There were just enough trees to block the view from the road. Before they got out of their car, I rolled my window down half way and waited for them to approach. Both teens walked toward my vehicle, eager to take turns at punching me in the face. When the male came to my window screaming and holding up his fists, I flipped him off again and waited for my opportunity. The girl was standing behind him, echoing his taunts. When he saw my middle finger again, it sent him over the edge. He brought his face to my window and yelled at me to get out of the car and fight like a man.

I casually grabbed his head with both hands, pulled him in and held him in position while Zach reached over and rolled the window up into his neck. When Zach had the guy locked in, I let go of his head and continued adding pressure to his neck until the glass had gone half way through his neck and blood was gushing down my door. I didn't realize you could do that with a car window – or perhaps I'm just stronger than I thought. I opened the door with his body hanging from it and chased after the girl, who had already made it back to their car. With tires spinning, she raced back toward Calumet in reverse. I bolted back to my vehicle and chased after her. Zach was up on his knees in excitement as the woman whipped her car around to turn right out of the gravel road heading forward. I had not planned any further than catching the witness and eliminating her. I wasn't even considering the fact that I might have been pulled over by police for speeding. I turned right to follow her, and the body detached from the head at my window, sending it into oncoming traffic while the head fell into my lap. I was startled at first because, I had almost forgotten that the guy was still hanging around.

I pursued the girlfriend at increasingly high speeds, weaving around cars to keep up. She turned left on 117th street but must have misjudged her speed, because she slid sideways and slammed into a car parked along the street. Afterwards, everything happened so quickly that I didn't have time to think. I parked across the street and began to walk toward her vehicle. I didn't know what I was going to do when I reached her, but I kept looking around for potential witnesses. While I was contemplating my next move, Zach sprinted around me and commenced to stabbing the woman with his knife until she was no longer screaming. I was bewildered by his sloppy behavior, intense laughter, and lack of consideration for possible bystanders. I yelled, "Hey, that's enough, let's go!" When Zach turned to comply, a woman in a silver family sedan pulled up behind me and asked, "Is everyone ok?" I immediately turned to the woman, and without forethought, shot her in the nose. We already had our backpacks on, so there was no reason to return to the SUV. I pushed the woman over while Zach jumped in on the passenger side, and we sped off.

Just as I began to wrap my mind around what had just happened, we noticed that a boy, aged about five in the back seat, crying. I didn't know what to do next, but I knew I didn't want to hurt the kid. He was young enough that he might not be able to identify me, so I decided I would just drop him off near a gas station somewhere. However, before I could even tell Zach my plan, he had climbed over the seat to better reach the boy and began to stab him in the stomach and chest. I flipped my mirror up so Zach could get it out of his system while I wasn't watching, but I will never forget those sounds. When he climbed back into the passenger seat, I just kept my silence, because I was pretty upset with my boy. While we were driving, *Don't Fear the Reaper* by Blue Oyster Cult came on, and the car was silent otherwise. The sun was going down, Zach and I were both covered in blood, and there was a kid's body in the back seat. I kept looking over at Zach during the song, and he kept a thousand mile stare while blood dripped from his chin. Time seemed to stop and everything felt perfect.

I don't remember what time we made it here last night, but we're in a corn field a couple miles before Lawndale, Illinois. I found enough grassy space between the field and wood line to drive through. From here, it shouldn't be much longer until we reach Springfield. The car is parked in the woods about 30 yards away from us, but I almost want to just keep walking, rather than get back into that car with a dead kid. I'll probably just end up leaving him in the woods though. I've been having some serious concerns about Zach's actions lately. He has been unpredictable and he doesn't think before he acts. I know he's only eight, but he tells me he will be nine next month, and that should be old enough to think before he acts. We had a long discussion about it last night. When I asked him why he'd killed the boy, he said I told him we can't have witnesses. I hated seeing it, but I guess Zach doing it wasn't as bad as me doing it. As for the teen girl in the car, he had the same no witness excuse. I told him he shouldn't do things when other people could be watching because that would just create more witnesses. He revealed me as a hypocrite when he reminded me that I had fired a gun in the middle of a residential area right after a car wreck.

My stomach sank when he mentioned that, because I knew he was right. I wasn't thinking either. There were probably several people that heard the gun, and some may have even seen me. My face will be all over the news; they will catch me and I will lose my Zach forever. Though he is unpredictable, everything he has done so far has been justified. His actions have kept us from being caught. Perhaps it isn't that he doesn't think before he acts, as much as it is that he thinks faster than I do. I held him tight as we slept between two rows of corn and I prayed to God that He wouldn't let us get caught. I promised Him that I would stop killing people and make a good life with my son. I swore to never harm another person as long as he could just help me along by letting me keep my freedom. It's funny how tragedy makes a person find God.

March 17, 2014 (11:45 a.m.) Lawndale, IL

N/A

Dear Diary, the authorities must really be looking hard for us, because I saw several police helicopters in the last couple hours. I don't understand why they are so worried about it though. It has nothing to do with them and all I'm doing is increasing the amount of oxygen and resources available to them by removing others from the picture. A little while ago, I decided to see if the coast was clear by lying in the woods near 55 and watching for law enforcement activity. I kept seeing the same police car travel back and forth in fifteen minute intervals. I'm under the impression that guards are stationed along different sections of the highway. I'm working on a plan to get out of here, and I believe we need to stay away from the roads.

March 18, 2014 (8:30 p.m.)   Evans, Illinois

N/A

Dear Diary, we planned to keep walking west along the creek to see where it would lead us. I realized that if the car was spotted in the woods, the whole area would be covered by police in no time. We returned to the car and drove close enough to the road to see the cop do his drive by, but distant enough to avoid detection. Once he passed, I quickly parked the car along the road and grabbed a double handful of coagulated blood from the back seat, while trying not to throw up. It's obviously not the blood that turned my stomach, but the image of a little kid lying in a pool of jelly blood with more stab wounds than a cutting board about did me in. I walked two car lengths in front of our car, and splattered the blood on the ground. I set the crime scene to appear that I abandoned one vehicle to hijack another. We then began following the creek.

I had no plans on what to do next, but I needed to keep Zach safe. We continued walking through what seemed to be miles of woods and fields, until we reached a large, white farmhouse in the middle of nowhere. At first I contemplated seizing the house with brute force. However, after further observation, I noticed a two story, rustic-looking red barn sitting behind the house. I hoped we could find a spot within the barn in which we could hide without being spotted by the owner, until things cooled down. There was an Amish man in his sixties feeding his horses in front of the barn doorway, so we had to wait until he returned back to his home. We were both getting anxious, due to the ridiculous amount of time the man spent just feeding his horses by hand. Why not just put the hay on the ground, or at least in a tub? I know he had to be a bit off in the head.

After he was gone, we traveled the wood line to the back of the barn, trying not to be spotted through a window. We ran to the barn and crept around to enter the front doorway. The horses noticed us, but didn't react to our presence. It seemed like the owner was a bit of a hoarder, so finding a place to stay wasn't going to be hard. The back wall had hay stacked over ten feet high and there was a wooden ladder nailed to the wall, leading to the second-story loft. We climbed the ladder to make a hideout behind some hay. When we reached the top, there was a partially decomposed woman lying on her back, with her clothes folded neatly beside her. Her skin was mostly purple and her belly was puffed out and hard to the touch. So yeah, I touched it. There were some parts of her body in which areas of the skin had started to peel away or rip. Her wide-open mouth was full of maggots, which were using holes in her cheeks as shortcuts to her ears. I can't tell how she died, but I wonder if the old man knows she's up here. After we studied the body for a while longer, Zach and I made our way past it and created a sleeping area behind a stack of bales. We should be safe up here for a couple days. It was hard to get Zach to sleep with the body so close. He wanted so badly to cut her open to see what was inside. I told him it was like anyone else's, but he was very insistent that she would have no organs left, and that she was probably a piñata full of maggots. I did eventually talk him out of his curiosity and he nodded off.

March 19, 2014 (9:55 a.m.)   Evans, IL

N/A

Last night was a little disturbing and I still haven't wrapped my mind around what I have witnessed, but at least we have a place to stay for a couple weeks. As Zach and I slept, I was awakened by creaking of the ladder as the old man made his way up to our location. I thought we'd been spotted and I assumed he would be bringing along a gun to kill us for trespassing. I pulled out my gun and crawled to the corner of our hay fort to watch him coming. What happened next was something I haven't ever seen before.

This Amish man, dressed in overalls, a top hat, and work boots, sat his lantern down by the head of the dead body. He then proceeded to remove his pants and make love to it. I tried not to watch, but I was strangely intrigued by this unusual behavior. My head was filled with questions, and I was wondering about my own future. Did this guy always have this affliction? Does he attempt to resist it? How and where did this all start? Did he start off like me and evolve into *this*? Is this what I am going to be doing when I am his age? I felt he could help me with my problem if he could only answer my questions. All I know is that I don't want to end up like him. I just want to live a normal life with my son. I can't end up like that.

As I watched, I felt a chin rest on my shoulder. Zach was apparently startled by the man's relentless moaning. I signaled for him to keep quiet as we patiently waited for the man to finish. If I was going to introduce myself to him, I didn't want to start it off by being rude. When I stood up and said "Hi", he jumped up and grabbed his lantern as if he was going to throw it at me. When Zach popped out, he lowered it and asked us what we wanted. I told him we weren't there to judge him, but rather to hide from the consequences of my own affliction. I let him know I would like to ask him some questions and asked if it was fine if we remained in the barn until the police stopped sniffing around.

He invited us into his home and cooked dinner for us. He prepared meat loaf and mashed potatoes. I can't believe how well he can cook. Of course, I probably should have guessed. We all sat around his kitchen table in silence as we ate our dinner. The inside of his house was surprisingly empty, being that his barn was piled wall to wall with assorted rubbish. The only thing in the kitchen besides the table was a wood burning stove, some old wall-mounted pictures of sheep, a pitchfork, and a dog bowl that contained a dried black substance. It was evident that he had no dog and that the bowl had been sitting in that same spot for quite some time. After we finished, he asked us to come to his living room, where he poured three glasses of whisky. He didn't even question Zach's age when he offered the boy a drink. Obviously, Zach was happy to accept, and so was I. It was funny watching my son struggle with the taste, of the whiskey, but he ended up pulling it off. Our host lit the fire place, which explained why the whole house smelled like a campfire. For about an hour, we all just sat around in wicker chairs staring at each other. There were very few words spoken. It was like the conversations were in the air, but not quite audible. I've never been so content with silence. My mind was racing with questions, but I didn't want to be rude.

He asked how many people we have killed so far and when I told him sixteen, he got a satisfied smile on his face. He then told me he stopped counting at ten and the three of us suddenly started to laugh, as if somebody had told a hilarious joke. I still don't know what was funny, but Zach actually spit out his whisky because he was laughing so hard. I think we all shared the same bonding sensation at that moment, and we remained silent for about another hour before anyone else spoke. We did make an occasional silly face at each other, but that's about it. The old man eventually told us we could stay as long as we liked, but he would need to be compensated for food. I told him I have plenty of money from our travels but he declined my offer. He said money isn't an issue for him, what he wanted was a new woman.

I promised that I would get our new friend a new girlfriend before we left, as long as he could guarantee that he would not harm Zach during our stay. He grinned and said he has no interest in boys anymore, so there's nothing to fear. He jokingly stated that if we were women, we wouldn't have made it out of his barn. We both laughed with him, but Zach's eyes were riddled with concern. It made me a little angry because I haven't seen that look in his eyes since Indiana. We need a place to lay low and as long as Zach isn't discovered to possess female genitalia, we should have no issues with our host. Besides his little addiction, he seems like a really nice guy. Plus, after everything we've been through, I'm more worried about the safety of the old man than I am for Zach.

March 19, 2014 (11:50 p.m.)   Evans, IL

N/A

Dear Diary, the old man's name is Abram, and he has been living on his own ever since his wife died – mysteriously, as he put it. He dresses Amish and rides a buggy, but I believe that could all be for presentation purposes because while helping him organize his basement, I noticed a little black and white television set hidden under a stack of blankets. I asked him if the Amish are allowed to watch television and he said no, but they aren't allowed to love the dead either. I asked him several questions while we were cleaning and he didn't shy away from answering them. In fact, he seemed to relish the fact that he finally had an open-minded audience to brag to. I asked him how he'd begun killing people. He said when he was a child, his father shot a horse that had broken its leg, and when he saw the horse die, he'd become instantly aroused. His father noticed his erection and sent him up to his room to read the Bible. He said that day was when he discovered that death gave him great joy.

He started off killing livestock, and when he was about sixteen, he even had sex with dead sheep because he couldn't handle excitement without action any longer. He said he tried to fight it, but always ended up just giving in. His younger brother had walked in on him while he was inside one of the sheep and had started to scream. Abram grabbed a pitch fork and ran it through the kid's back as he turned to run back toward the house. As his brother gasped for his final breaths, Abram became even more aroused. He ripped off his brothers pants and had sex with him while holding on to the pitch fork for support. He said he finished the rest of his family off that evening, one at a time, until he was the only one left in the house. He buried them all and told any visitors his family had decided to leave, but he didn't want to go with them. It was recognized in the community that the house and all other possessions were passed to him.

I can't believe that no one investigated his claims, but I realize there is much about his weird culture that is a mystery to me. All I know is that they make some really tasty cheese. I recognized that Abram's sexual desire for the dead began on day one, so that brought me some relief. I currently have no real sexual cravings at all, so I think I'll be able to cross "having sex with a corpse" from my list of things to expect in the future. When Zach walked down the steps, I changed the subject, because I'm trying to be a better role model for him. He sat on the bottom step for a while and listened to us talk about farming and wood carving. It felt nice to have something else to think about for a moment. When Abram walked into the next room, Zach asked, "I wonder if he has a staple gun." I couldn't help but to laugh at his quick-witted, inside joke.

March 22, 2014 (1:30 p.m.)   Hell

Zach?

What the fuck, Diary, I don't know what to do. I'm sitting here on the bed staring at a pool of blood on the floor. I think it belongs to Zach; it has to be Zach's. I've searched the whole house, the barn, and the fields. I'm about to explode and I'm starting to lose control. I woke up this morning and he's gone, along with Abram. I'm not sure what to do. I can't leave. What if they come back? What if it's a misunderstanding? What if something happened to Zach and Abraham is just taking him to the hospital? Who the fuck am I kidding? That old bastard has Zach and is probably fucking his body right now and I'm just sitting here crying, which is definitely a first for me. I don't know what to do, Diary. Do I call the police? Shit, there's already a search for Heather. I can't call the police. Damn damn damn. I'm blowing this fucking house up and I'm going to find that dead cunt fucking wrinkly waste of space. I'm done, I'm soooo fucking done!!

Yesterday morning Zach came to me after his shower with a look of fear on his face. He said that Abram walked in the bathroom while he was undressing. He said that Abram looked surprised, and then walked out. He said that we need to kill the old man and that he would have done it then, but he's going to start waiting on me to make those decisions. What the fuck, Diary. Why did I think I could make decisions? Zach knew what was right; I should have listened to him. Well, I told Zach that we would see how things go and if Abram acted weird, I'd kill him. The whole day, everything went as normal. Abram made the meals and we cleaned up the mess. We even helped tend to the animals. Abram said nothing out of the ordinary. I assumed that he had bad eyesight and hadn't actually seen that Zach was actually Heather. I thought that he might not have seen anything. I thought we were fine. I thought we could stay here until things cooled down and we would get him another woman before we left. I thought I would grow old and have Zach in my life forever. I was done killing. I was really trying to be done with killing. I needed Zach as my rock. He … Damn it, she's *Heather*, not Zach. Why am I still trying to hide behind the disguise? She's gone. The only person who has ever made me feel anything is gone. My child is gone. My future is gone. I can't even see her face. I close my eyes and I can't fucking see her face! That old motherfucker will suffer!

March something 2014   Here

I'm here, Diary, it's just me. The darkness has set in and I can't seem to find my way out. It's like I'm in a tunnel trying to find my way into the light. I haven't eaten for several days because I'm disgusted by the thought of food. The same thoughts keep circling around and around in my head. I sat out at the end of the driveway for a little over a day, just lying in the bushes with an axe, waiting for Abram to return. I know Heather is gone – or I *think* she is gone. What is gone? I don't know if she is gone. I just need Abram dead. I think he will return. It's his house, so he has to come back sometime. I'm not sure of the date because I don't give a fuck about the date. The date is just a timestamp and we only have so many stamps until we have to clock out for good. I killed a horse today and it did nothing for me. I have to find a way to feel normal again. My stomach is on fire. I walked the horse into the house and cut it open on the bastard's bed. I can't wait for him to see that shit. I'm probably going to leave all of his animals dead all around his house. Maybe he got arrested and he's in jail right now. What if the cops come here and I'm here. Do they know who I am?

March Something 2   Here?

Heather, please come back to me, I can't breathe anymore. I have to end it, if this is what I am to feel like for now on. I ate something from the fridge and I don't know what it was, but it helped alleviate the burning. I tried to walk down the street to find a town and ask around about Abram, but I never made it fifty feet from the end of the driveway because I still feel like they will be back and we can go back to normal. I'll clean with Heather and Abram will cook and I'll stab him in the fucking liver with a screwdriver like I should have done a while back. I'm about to go though. I have to pick up where I left off. I know that Heather would want me to stay on track. I know she would want me to continue our expedition. There's an annoying old cuckoo clock in the front room that fucks with my head every hour. It makes a knocking sound before the retarded little blue bird tries to escape. I always think someone is at the door. I would destroy it, but it's my only friend. I don't know me, man.

Today   In a Closet

Crawling in circles attempting to play
Babies are born to sleep in a grave
It's hopeless to seek and search out a purpose
When time is useless and humans are worthless
Tracking them down and thinning them out
My life is mine and theirs as well
I'll spend my spend nights in prep for hell

Another Day   On the Porch

Why am I so diluted and confused? I don't know what is happening to me. I feel like *me*, but then it fades. I stare into the field and wish I had never left my home. I wonder what my family is up to these days. Oh fuck! The damn bird just knocked again. Where was I? Yeah, I wonder if they worry that I'm dead. Perhaps I will just return to them and start over. The same scenes keep looping in my head and I can't stop the cycle. I know that no matter what I think in my head, the world isn't going to be impacted by it. I keep seeing Abram fucking Heather's lifeless body. I keep telling myself that she may have killed him instead and that she's just lost. I keep walking up and down the driveway. I always just walk the driveway. I noticed most of the animals are dead now? Was it me or did they starve? I don't know anymore. I'm pretty much giving up hope, I need to move on. I need to forget. I need to realize that these kinds of emotions are not for me.

Nightfall   On the Couch

I had to cut my arm today because I didn't feel alive. I was just sitting at the table staring at a knife and my mind went blank. It was like I wasn't even here and that the arm I was looking at was one from a corpse. I committed to three cuts on the top of my forearm – from my wrist to my elbow. When I realized what I was doing, and how deep the wounds were, I quickly grabbed a couple shotgun shells from the gun rack drawer. I remembered that in a movie, I saw someone dump gun powder in their wound and light it to stop the bleeding. Well that's what I tried. It didn't work as well as it did on the movies and I still had to wrap my arm tightly with a towel.

Morning   Bathroom

I'm trying to control my emotions. I don't know how I ended up here. I think I've been a pretty good person and I've only been doing what I have been created to do. Why would God do this to someone who is just trying to help eliminate the evil in this world? Maybe there's nothing there after all. Maybe I'll shoot myself and get it over with.

I remember when I was a child and the burden of feelings and emotions wasn't a problem. My mom understood me. I was pulled from school for a fight in fifth grade and was homeschooled from there on out. I was just your average back-of-the-class, quiet boy and when other kids picked on me, I never gave them the attention they craved. I felt the kicks in the shins and flips in the back of the head, but it wasn't that bad. I knew they didn't like me, but I wasn't interested in figuring out why.

It never made me sad or depressed. I never felt anything at all. I miss those days. It wasn't my decision to be pulled from school. My mom always told me that I was normal and that I was just misunderstood. I guess if it was a routine fifth grade fight, I could have remained in school. There was a boy in my grade who was recognized as the lead bully. One day, during recess, he tried to kick my legs and ended up tripping me. When I fell, I hit my face on the ground and it made my nose bleed. When I arose and wiped my nose with my arm, the sight of my own blood sent me into a rage. I tackled the bully to the ground, climbed on his chest, dug my thumbs into his eyes and began biting his arms that were trying to pull my hands from his face. The only thing I remember afterward is that the boy was taken away by ambulance and I was escorted into the principal's office to write a police report while I waited on my mom to pick me up. I didn't understand why they were making a fifth grader fill out a police report. I didn't understand why everyone was so upset about my actions. In my head, I was justified.

June 1, 2014 (6:05 p.m.)   Wausau, WI

Family of 3 (19)

Dear Diary, I can't begin to explain how embarrassed I should feel about my behavior lately. I can't believe I let myself feel emotions for someone. It was like I was locked up in a cave and when I finally walked out, I was sleeping in a strange family's bathtub with their heads bobbing around me. It was a man who looked about 40, a woman around the same age, and a girl about 16. I think that's what woke me up. That is actually the only way I can begin to explain it – I just woke up. I felt like a normal person again. Well, my version of normal anyway. I realize now that I will never see Heather again, so I've finally been able to block out the emotions that were keeping me tormented. I didn't realize how much time had gone by until I dried off and noticed that I'd lost about 50 pounds. I found the living room where the bodies were still sitting straight up on the couch. I sat down between them and checked the news for any information on Heather. They were still talking about all of my murders, but it seems that everyone thinks I'm done. Well, I'm far from done; I'm just getting started. I don't give a fuck anymore. I am filled with hate and rage, which until recently were sensations I was only slightly familiar with. I'm not fighting it, and I no longer care if I get caught because if I do get caught, I'll kill every cell mate I get until *they* finally kill *me*. I watched the television for hours with my new family, and when the date flashed up on the screen, I felt like I had time-traveled. I still thought it was March, or at the most, the beginning of April. I didn't realize I had spent over two months drowning myself in sorrow.

The longer I sat still, the more I began to wonder how I even got here. I didn't even know where here was until I rummaged through the kitchen drawers and found some mail. I remember getting a ride from someone, but I don't think I killed them. I think it was a truck driver… Yeah, it was a truck driver. He was heading north and I hitched a ride with him and that's how I got here; but what about the bodies? How was I able to kill three people sitting on the couch and have them still remain vertical? I can't remember that piece of time, no matter how hard I try, so I gave up. I feel normal, but different. I can't really explain it; it's like I had no reason to live in the beginning of all of this, but now I feel that I have a strong purpose on this earth. I feel important and I feel empowered. I'm supposed to kill the world and everyone in it. If I can't do that, I'm supposed to take out as many as I can before I die. My urge is stronger than it has ever been, and all humans are parasites in my eyes now. I think my lust to kill Abram for so long has ignited a flame in my soul that was just waiting to be lit.

June 3, 2014 (5:00 p.m.)   Saint Paul, MN

Campers (51)

Dear Diary, I've been having a little bit of fun for the past couple days. I discovered that I really enjoy camping. I spent the night in the house with my headless family to regroup and try to assess my situation. I found a Smith & Wesson handgun under the dresser in the master bedroom. I was very excited, because under the bed were several boxes of ammunition. I don't think I ever have to worry about running out of bullets now. I dug through my bag to find my old gun, and shoved it under the dresser. I won't miss it because it was about out of bullets. I wiped the handle really good, because I don't want Heather's prints on a weapon, just in case she is still alive. While looking through the bag, I might have uncovered a bit of a problem. I noticed Heather's hair was still in the bottom from when I cut it off. It made my chest sink, and when I looked up, the whole house was destroyed. The TV, windows, and anything glass was broken. The fridge was knocked over and the couch was on fire, burning the bodies. It startled me because I didn't remember doing any of it. That's actually the reason I left the house. I thought about throwing the hair away if it makes me blank out, but I can't get rid of the only thing I have to remember Heather by.

Well, I'll get to why I love camping so much. When I left the house, I walked down Maple Street searching for transportation. It was about 8:00 a.m. and I noticed a man strapping a kayak onto the top of his brown sedan. I also saw that there were no neighbors walking around. There was a little girl in the back seat and a woman that I think must have been mom sitting in the passenger seat. The man walked back into the house, and I seized the moment. I ran and jumped into the back seat of the car with the child and aimed the gun at her head. I then told the mom to keep her mouth shut if she wanted her daughter to live. It took everything she had not to scream, but she was able to resist – under the circumstances. The man was walking back, holding several fishing poles and smoking a cigar. Who the hell smokes cigars? He didn't even look in to see me as he loaded the poles into the trunk. He then walked up, climbed in the driver's seat and started checking his pockets for his keys. He turned to see his wife in distress and said, "What's wrong?" She said nothing, and then he looked in the back seat. Dude jumped and screamed like a newborn woman. I replied with, "Hi dad, where are we heading?" He saw the gun and knew that he had to tread lightly.

He said we were heading to Chippewa Falls to go camping near a lake. I told him it sounded like a plan to me and I sat back with my arm around the girl, relaxing while we drove to the campground. I couldn't help but to pick up on a bit of uneasiness in the air as both parents kept looking in the mirrors and at each other. During the couple hour trip he asked why I was doing this. I told him that I just tried to rob a convenience store and the police were after me. His daughter was a little brown haired girl of about 10, and she sort of reminded me of Heather. I decided then, that I would try to replace Heather and hopefully fill the void in my soul. When we arrived at the camping area, we pulled along the woods where there was a line of about 40 tents. The dad told me I could leave and no one would say anything about what happened, or about the store. He even offered to pay me, assuming my hard knock robbery sob story was true. I decided to trust that he wouldn't call the cops. I told him that I would leave and since no one was hurt they should all keep their mouths shut. I told them that if I found out the cops were looking for me near the campground, I would kill them in their sleep. I reminded them that I knew where they live. They promised to keep quiet and I ran off into the woods.

I found a thicket to hide in while I waited for nightfall. Once the darkness set in, I made my way back to the edge of the woods behind their tent. I listened in, as they were still talking about me. The mom seemed determined to report the incident, but the dad kept telling her that he thinks they should leave it alone and keep their mouths shut. He said that he didn't believe my robbery tale and thinks that I'm the traveler killer that's all over the news. He said it fits my profile because that's how the traveler got to some of his victims. He said that they got lucky and that they need to just forget it ever happened. I was thinking to myself how smart he was to make a decision like that. However, I began to rethink my thoughts about getting caught. If I'm going to kill as many people as possible, I can't be getting caught this early. Therefore, I realized I would have to kill them that night.

I didn't know how late people stayed up when they were camping, but most of the campground finally fell silent a few hours before sunrise. I walked quietly up to their tent and attempted to unzip it, but the zipper was much too loud for the level of stealth required. I looked around for some kind of blade, because I seemed to have misplaced mine somewhere. I found a hatchet / pick axe next to a neighboring tent, sitting on a cooler. This was perfect because it was razor sharp. I came back to the tent and quietly sliced a line in the back big enough for me to slip through. All three were lying there so peacefully. I struck the dad in the top of the head and the crack was louder than I expected. I remained silent for a couple minutes to make sure I didn't wake anyone. After I was sure everyone was still sleeping, I turned my attention to the mom but I didn't want it to be as loud. I had to crawl out and make another hole on her side of the tent. From the side, I hit her in the mouth with the spiked end of the hatchet, which went completely through and contacted the ground. Her eyes opened, but no sounds escaped. I thought she was alive for a minute – but I was wrong. I crawled into the tent further to reach the daughter. I raised the hatchet and stared at her for a minute before remembering that I was going to replace Heather. I mean, how hard can it be? I held my hand over her mouth and told her to wake up. She attempted to scream but I showed her the hatchet and she became compliant.

I held my hand to the girl's mouth and helped her rise to a sitting position. She noticed her dead parents and fainted. That's not what Heather did, but I thought that if maybe if I train her in the same way, this girl could still replace her. When she woke up, she was shivering and whimpering like a little baby. I told her I would spare her life but she needed to take my hatchet and shove the pointed end into the dad's chest. She refused so I took her hand and assisted her. Instead of continuing on her own like my Heather, she dropped down and began crying on his neck. I got a little mad because she wasn't doing as I directed. I decided that there was still hope, but she would just take longer to get used to her new life than Heather did. I took her by the hand and had her follow me to the next tent. I thought that she would feel better about killing if she didn't know the person. I sliced the side of the tent and inside was a younger male couple, in their twenties. I whispered for the girl to keep her mouth shut because I was about to kill these guys and I didn't want to wake anyone else up. I hit the first guy in the mouth with the blade end, hoping to just separate the head, but the teeth made it difficult. The hatchet only made it half way in and the guy start to gurgle loudly. I quickly retracted the blade and hit him again in the throat. This woke his partner and I had to hit him in the head before he made too much noise. The crack was loud and I had to sit in silence for a few moments.

I turned to bring the girl in and she was lying on the ground – fucking passed out again. I quickly realized that Heather must have been special, and I wasn't going to find a replacement. She must have been born with the same affliction I suffer from but just didn't realize it yet. I figured I'd just end it for the girl and move on to the next tent, but while I looked at her asleep I couldn't bring myself to do it. I don't get it. I'm so full of hate and I need to kill the world, but why can't I hurt a kid? There's no way to kill the world without killing its children as well. Oh well, after my camping trip, I give up on killing everyone in my path. I will stick to adults, but I will not honor my initial plans to only kill when I feel the urge, because I *always* feel the urge. There is no longer anything that can take my pain. Killing seems to help a little but it's only for minutes rather than days like it used to be, and to a far lesser extent.

Well, back to my camping experience. I found some duct tape in the back of the guy's jeep, which I used to tape the girl's mouth and wrap her body like a cocoon so she couldn't raise the alarm. I repeated the same open and chop routine for about an hour or so, until I'd claimed the lives of 32 people. I had to skip a couple tents because people were still talking within. After my final tent, I found some keys and took their truck. That's how I made it here. I took 29 W to 94 W pretty much the whole way to Saint Paul. I'm just sitting here at a Park trying to get my thoughts on paper while I try to think of where I'm going to spend the night.

My hands are almost too sore to keep writing to you but I have to keep going. I think I'm going to get a couple blisters from all of the hatchet action I've been getting. I wonder what will come of you, Diary, after I am dead, or in prison. Will others read you? And if they do, will any of them be able to relate to me? I wonder if anyone will be sitting on their couch just wishing they could have joined me on my journey? I wonder if there is at least one person that could relate to my anger? Perhaps they may vent through my experiences and feel what I have felt. I know at the very least, you will end up as evidence.

June 4, 2014 (11:50 p.m.)   Saint Paul, MN

2 Waiters (53)

Dear Diary, I sat at the park for a couple hours until I realized how hungry I was. I honestly cannot remember the last time I had eaten, which could explain how I lost so much weight. I can't complain, though because this is the first time I've ever been skinny. I drove up Chestnut Street to find the local hospital and ditched my vehicle in a nearby parking lot, trying to avoid letting any cameras see my face. I continued walking until I reached a steak house and decided I earned the right to splurge a little. I was hoping to relax enough to get the constant ringing out of my ears. I don't know when that started, but it's getting on my nerves. I sat at the booth in the back corner of the restaurant and stared out the window. The city reminded me of a large ant hill in which there is no way out; everyone is busy, and nothing really gets accomplished. When the waitress came, I had difficulty making out her words. I think the ringing was interfering with the annoyingly high-pitched tone of her voice. I ended up ordering a steak with fries and a double shot of whiskey. The way she was looking at me led me to believe she knew who I was. I could tell she was judging me and that she wanted me dead. Well, I didn't want to wait around for her to make the first move.

I ate about half of my steak and I couldn't eat anymore. I guess my stomach has to get used to eating again. I wrapped the other half in a napkin and stuffed it into my backpack for later. Afterward, I went to the bathroom because I wasn't sure how to kill the waitress who couldn't stop staring at me. She asked me if I wanted anything else eight times during my meal because she just wanted to keep an eye on me, I knew it. Since it was about closing time before I was done eating, I found a dumpster in the back near the employee parking lot to hide in and wait. The plan was to peak out of the lid and hope that she would walk to her car by herself so I could take her out with my handy dandy what?… yeah, hatchet. It didn't exactly work out as planned, but it was still beautiful. I heard the back door open and it was her voice that I heard going toward the dumpster, grumbling about her boss. I guess she had trash duties and didn't care for it very much. When she threw the dumpster door open, I reacted by popping up like a deranged jack in the box, grabbing her by the face, and pulling her in while muffling her mouth with my hand. The dumpster door slammed shut behind us while I held her down against the mounds of trash bags and random scraps of old food. I held her mouth shut and leaned forward to whisper in her ear. I told her to remain silent and that every word she said would be another stab wound.

I stared into her eyes, which were made dimly visible by the streetlights shining through the holes in the dumpster lid. I suddenly remembered my stepfather and how good it felt to watch the life leave his eyes. I knew I needed to witness the same thing with her. While we laid there making eye contact, I was startled by the sound of someone else walking toward the dumpster. I held my finger to my mouth to signal for her to hush as I slowly removed my hand and reached for my hatchet. As soon as the door opened, I stood up and struck a young man of about 19 in the temple with the pointed pick end and pulled him forward, to bring him into the dumpster with us. The waitress attempted to scream, so I shoved my two middle fingers into her mouth and down her throat far enough so that she was trying to bite my knuckles as she gasped for air. Her body was shaking frantically and she began gagging, which made her vomit. It sprayed through my fingers and out of her mouth but I still held her in place and kept her face up. With her mouth full of regurgitated steak and my fingers shoved in her esophagus, she stopped breathing. I lowered my face to her eyes to watch and she attempted to close them. I held one eye open with my other hand said, "You better fuck'n look at me." I got to watch her eye go dull and her body relax. Death has to be the most peaceful experience in the world because no matter how hysterical you are before you die; afterward, your body goes completely limp and your worries instantly disappear.

After I was able to clean the vomit from my face and hands with the girl's shirt I peered out of the dumpster to see if there was anyone else in the area. Once I was comfortable that the coast was clear, I dug in her pockets to retrieve her key chain. I jumped out and began trying all of the employee's car doors until I found the right one. It was a little white VW Beetle that reminded me of a show I used to like when I was younger. I didn't know where I would spend the night but I was just happy to be away from that restaurant. Well, I *didn't* know, that is, until I found the waitress's address on a piece of junk mail. She lived just across the river, on a road called Manomin Ave. I parked in front of her house and reclined the seat as I watched the windows, waiting to see what I was up against. It was a two story house with vinyl siding and a tall hedge along the right side. The time was about 10pm and there was only one faint blue light coming from the front room, which turned out to be a television. There was a window on the side of the house beside the hedge. I was able to get a glimpse of a man sleeping on the couch. The window was unlocked, so I decided I would go in and take the guy out. Just as I got half way into the window, I heard sirens. I didn't know if they were for the dumpster bodies but it suddenly hit me that the first place the police would come is to her house. I climbed back out the window and ran to the car. After I shut the door behind me, I realized that every police department in the area would be searching for it. I left the Beetle parked in front of the house and ran down the street looking for another place to sleep.

I made it to a park, where I'm planning to spend the night here in the woods. I'm glad it is a clear moonlit night or I wouldn't have been able to make it through the trees. The sounds of sirens and helicopters are coming from everywhere. I'm feeling pretty boxed in right now but I'm sure everything will be better in the morning. I keep entertaining the thought that Heather might be alive and I wonder if there's any way I could find her. However, based on Abram's background, I'm sure she's gone. I think I'll just stay on my path for a couple more months and return to his house. Maybe after such a long time, he will believe I'm gone for good and I could sneak in on him. If we ever cross paths again, I will make him suffer. I wonder how much skin I could remove with a cheese grater before he dies.

June 6, 2014 (1:30p.m.)   Saint Paul, MN?

2 Cops (55)

Dear Diary, I thought I would get a chance to sleep last night but I was wrong. I didn't expect them to pull out the dogs. As I began to doze off, I heard dogs barking from different locations in the woods and I knew it was the police trying to zero in on me. I jumped up, pulled the gun from my bag, and began running away from the sounds. I came to the edge of the woods next to the river and I had to stop because there were two police officers with a bloodhound walking about 30 yards away on the path between me and the river. It became clear to me how much of a wanted man I was. I guess it makes sense, because it's not that common to kill over 50 people and remain free. I crossed my fingers, hoping that they would just keep walking, but the damn dog took a right turn and started coming my way. I didn't know what else to do so I took off my shirt and hung it on a tree branch beside me and took a piss all over the tree. I then hid behind a large rock that was about 10 feet away from the tree. As they got closer I never got anxious or nervous. I don't even think my heart rate went up much. I knew I didn't want to get caught yet, but I didn't really care if I did either. As they approached the tree, the cops had their guns sighted in. The dog kept on walking, toward the smell of the tree and he passed right in front of me. One cop noticed the corner of my shirt sticking out and nudged his partner while pointing toward it. They approached cautiously as I walked from behind the rock and shot both of them in the back of the head. I scurried to the tree to reclaim my shirt and had to shoot the dog as well. I didn't think the dog deserved to die, but he was determined that it was going to be me or him and well, it was him.

I ran to the river, jumped in, and started to drift down stream. Every couple minutes, I had to go under water because a helicopter light would be shining upon the water close to me. I was lucky I didn't drown, because the current was a little ridiculous. As I began to run out of energy, a large log hit me in the shoulder and I grabbed ahold of it. I rested my bag on the log, hoping that the water wouldn't get in and ruin my Diary. I later discovered that my bag was still dry inside, even though it was submerged several times; it must be waterproof or something. Anyway, I drifted the current for a while, until I came near a dam and I had to let go of the log and swim toward the bank. There were people standing along the dam, shining lights around in the water. I guess they figured I might try to take the river. I made it to the bank and took off into the woods once more. I was beginning to get really mad at their determination to capture me. I came to a housing project on 122 St but I didn't know if I was in the same town or not. I was going to enter a house, but they were really big and all had several cars. I figured they would also have alarms and I didn't know how many people would be inside; plus in houses that big, people could be hidden in rooms all over the place. There's no way I could feel comfortable that I would be free of witnesses. I found a tree house that was actually built like a mini mansion and I decided to sleep there for the night, to let things cool off.

As I squeezed in through the front door of the tree house I heard snoring. I crawled around the corner to see two boys about 11 having a camp out or something. Nevertheless, I wondered why the parents were locked up in a secure house while their most valuable assets were laying out here in the open. I pulled out my hatchet, but quickly put it back as I reminded myself that I'm unable to take out kids. But, I had to argue the point if a 16 year-old-girl was technically a child? So, where is my line? I wondered if it was 11, so I took my hatchet back out and crawled to the side of their bed and raised it in the air. I said 1, 2, 3, go several times in my head but I never did. I put it back in my bag and thought that 11 must still be too young. Perhaps 15 or 16 was my line. Whatever, I still needed a place to sleep without witnesses and it hit me that the kids probably knew all the house information I needed in order to get in. And maybe one of them could replace Zach.

I woke the boys one at a time by putting my hand over their mouth and tapping them in the forehead with the barrel of my gun. They awoke startled, but quickly became silent once they were aware of their situation. I explained to them that I didn't want to kill them, but I would. I told them that they had to choose between their lives or the lives of the people in the house. One began tearing up, because it was his family inside. The other was scared, but didn't seem as affected because he was just a visitor with no attachments to those inside. They both agreed that they valued their lives over the parents inside. The first boy said that inside the house were his mom, dad, and little sister. I told him his sister wouldn't be harmed, but his parents won't be waking up in the morning. I also told him that he shouldn't feel bad because it's their fault he was even in this mess in the first place. He cried and said he didn't think he could do it. I put the gun in his mouth and said, "Ok, your choice." He pulled back and agreed to do as I said.

As we walked toward the back of the house, a motion detector light came on and I aimed my face toward the ground and asked the boys if they had cameras. The first boy answered *no,* as he unlocked the back door and switched off the alarm. He began pleading with me to spare his parents' lives. I knew by his eyes that he wasn't going to be the one to replace Zach, and he may scream when he saw his parents die, which could wake his sister. I didn't want to complicate things any further, so I promised him that if they both sat outside the bedroom door and remained silent I would just wake his parents to ask them for a ride, and then I would leave. He signed with an extreme look of relief, and led me to his parents' door, pointing his sister's door out on the way. I let myself into the parents' room and shut the door quietly behind me. Approaching with my hatchet in hand, I started to think that I might be able to use these people for a while before killing them.

I opened the door to allow the boys inside, telling them that the parents would listen better with them present. I had them stand beside me and I switched out the hatchet for the gun. I turned on the light and said nothing. The dad put his arm over his eyes and the mom sat up, rubbing hers. I told her *hi,* and both parents jumped up in alarm, at the sound of strange man's voice in their bedroom. They noticed that I was aiming my gun at the boys and they asked me what I wanted. I told them that all I wanted was absolute cooperation, and no one would get hurt. I also told them that I had killed several others, and that I would not think twice to end their lives if they tried anything funny. I said that as long as I'm in their house, I will have a kid by my side and I will be in command. Plus, if anyone slips away to grab a phone or weapon, the kid closest to me will die without any hesitation on my part. They didn't see through my bluff, so they agreed. I also told them that their daughter is not to know about the situation, and that I would keep my weapon concealed so she would believe the story that I am a family friend. No reason to scar yet another child.

June 7, 2014 (10:15 a.m.)   Hastings, MN

Dear Diary, I'm still in the house with the Vanhorns. They gave me a bit of the cold shoulder in the beginning, but I think everything will work out fine for me while I'm here. I haven't slept yet, because something tells me that I can't completely trust them. I feel a new energy with everyone in the house being afraid of me. I don't think they have ever expressed their love for each other as much as they have since my arrival. They just huddle together on the floor, while I sit on their white couch, still soaked in river water. They keep asking what I want, but I just tell them I'd figure that out soon enough.

I knew I had to take a shower but I couldn't let anyone out of my sight. I had to take everyone into the bathroom with me. I made the kids stand in the corner by the door and the dad sit on the toilet. I made the mom wash my body, with the gun aimed at her forehead. It was the best I have felt since before Heather disappeared. Watching the family cry and beg made me all-powerful. Seeing the woman's face as she scrubbed the bloodstains from my neck, witnessing the coward of a dad struggle with his emotions while his wife washed another man's balls; I just started laughing at where I had ended up in life. Controlling people is almost better than killing them, but I don't think it would have been as fun if I was actually planning to let them live.

I am still not exactly sure what I am going to do from this point, but I think I'm going to test the human survival instinct a little. I've always wondered how much someone would do to save their own life, or if they would actually die for someone they loved. I have heard people promising others that they would take a bullet for them–but would they really? I began pondering this after the second boy received a call from his mother telling him it was time to come home. I had him beg to spend another night, but I considered the idea of having him lure her in for me. I wondered if he would have given his parents up as fast as Boy One did. Speaking of Boy One, his dad keeps calling him Billy. I had to put a stop that – quick. I told the dad that his name is Boy One and he is named Dad. I told them all that I don't need to hear their names. It is annoying, time consuming to remember, and pointless. The girl kept coming over to me asking me tons of questions and tried to get me to play games with her. I know she's too young to be Heather. If I expose both of the boys to Zach's lifestyle, I wonder if one of them would be able to fill the void of my missing child. As everyone slept on the living room floor, I realized I would be staying for a while.

June 8, 2014 (1:00 p.m.)   Hastings, MN

Dad's Co-worker (56)

Dear Diary, since my last entry, much has developed in the life of the Vanhorns. I have decided I will be more successful in killing more people with this method than any of my previous ones. While sitting around watching television, there was an alert about me on nearly every channel. They have pinned me with over 40 murders, according to the little man with the funny tie. The family trembled as I shouted at the TV, "It's fifty-five, you fucking idiots!" All of them began to cry and beg for their lives once they knew who I was. Well, everyone except the girl. She didn't realize anything and was only concerned that her parents were concerned. I told them I wanted to do an experiment and that if they passed my tests, I would leave them alone. I asked for the dad's cell phone and he obviously obliged. He had over 200 contacts and I told him that we were going to have a party. I told him to call one person from his list that he knew would come to a spontaneous cookout. I said that I would be killing that person and that he could refuse at the cost of his wife's life. So basically, he just had to find someone he loves less than his wife. Seems easy right? Well, he scrolled through the names trying his best to narrow it down as his wife looked him as if his decision was taking too long. He just kept murmuring, "This isn't really happening."

He finally decided to go with a co-worker. He called him and said that he was having a cookout and would love for him to come. He mentioned that he shouldn't bring the kids because there was a lot of drinking taking place. I thought that was pretty intelligent of the dad, to not put any more children in the picture. I only wish I'd thought of it first. When he hung up the phone, I asked him how he'd decided on this specific individual. He said that they were going after the same job. When the man arrived holding a case of beer, my mouth started to water. He asked where everyone was and the dad told him he was the first to arrive. I was introduced as a friend of the family, and I went along with it. It's funny, because this guy was being sacrificed for a career opportunity. I'm not sure who the bad guy is in this

house.
When the guest opened the refrigerator to put in the beer, I chopped the back of his head with the hatchet, dropping him instantly. Everyone screamed and ran around in a panic. I didn't tell them to quit or to shut up. I just stood there observing their reaction. The dad was torn up with guilt because seeing death in real life, and just hearing about it are two different worlds. After they were done throwing their fits, I had the dad wrap the man in a blanket and the mom clean up the mess. I then focused my attention on the kids, who were – all three – hiding in the girl's closet. I told them the girl can stay but one boy must remain with me at all times as we'd agreed. No one wanted to come, so I chose Boy One, since I wanted to train him. I took him to the basement, where dad had placed the body. I gave the kid my hatchet and asked him to strike the body. He refused, so I took his hand and assisted him. He started crying uncontrollably and pleaded for me to stop. He finally took off running up the stairs. I followed behind, pissed at his disobedience. I knew that I would have to give up on finding my Heather replacement, and that filling the void with bodies would have to be good enough. I also realize that I was a little deluded when I thought I could kill the world. It sounds fun, but it is physically impossible. Traveling the States doesn't even appeal to me anymore, but I will do as much traveling as I can in the memory of my Zach.

June 8, 2014 (10:30 p.m.)   Hastings, MN

Dad & Mom Vanhorn (58)

Dear Diary, I am about to head out, because it will only be a matter of time before *they* find out I'm here. I'm sure the gunshot was heard by the neighbors. After the co-worker's death, I told the mom it was her turn. She picked a name from her contacts. I asked her who it was, and she said it was someone from her soccer carpool. I assumed it was another mom that she didn't like. I caught onto their pattern and decided to just pick for myself. People will obviously sacrifice the ones they don't know or don't like, but I want to know what they will do when choosing between two loved ones. I picked the name 'Dad' from her phone, and she began to freak out. This is what I've been looking for. She got mad and started cussing at me. I soaked it up for a couple minutes then pulled the gun on the dad and said, "Your choice, you snobby, fat bitch!" Everyone fell silent as she took the phone from me. She called him, crying and she couldn't get the words out. She broke down and hung up the phone. I lowered the gun, went to the kitchen, grabbed a large knife, and stuck it in her chest. The dad tried to charge me and I welcomed his advance by smacking him across the face with my gun. Everyone was in a real panic now, and the volume of their sorrow seemed to lighten my mood a little. Well, by now the girl had finally figured out that I was not actually a friend of the family after all. She kept screaming and throwing things at me. The boys were crying too, but they attempted to calm her down, thinking I would turn on her – LOL.

I handed the phone to Boy Two and told him that he needed to have his mom pick him up, and that I would kill her upon her arrival. His body went limp and he dropped to his knees and pleaded for me to stop. I told him it was him or her, and he surprised me by his response. He said, "Just take me, because I'm not giving you my mom!" I had to walk away to gather my thoughts. I didn't know what to do after that. I guess I could have killed him if I really tried, but it would have been difficult for me. I was amazed by his willingness to sacrifice himself for his mom at only about 11 or 12 years old. I asked him if he would accompany me on my journey if I spared him and his mom. He said he would do whatever I wanted. I gave him the knife and said, "Stab your friend." The dad was in a ball beside his dead wife and was oblivious to the conversation I was having with the children. Boy One began screaming, "No, please no!" I was just testing to see if Boy Two would do it; I didn't really want to see Boy One die, but I then remembered his previous failure to comply, which made it seem a little more justified. Boy Two told his friend he was sorry and pulled back the knife to strike him. Suddenly I remembered Zach killing the kid in the back seat of the car, and how it had turned my stomach. I grabbed the kid's hand and said, "No, the dad." Boy One basically passed out from his rollercoaster of emotions. As ordered, Boy Two walked up beside the distraught dad and stabbed him in the side. The dad reacted by jumping up and striking the boy. I immediately shot the dad in the face, and helped young Eddie to his feet. He was crying, so I tried to comfort him by saying, "Don't feel bad, if I would have given him the knife, he would have stabbed you to save his son." Well, at least that's what I assumed would have happened, since that was going to be my next test if Eddie had failed.

June 9, 2014 (11:25 p.m.)   Bismarck, ND

Woman (59)

Dear Diary, Eddie is no Zach or Heather, but he has come in useful. I don't think I'll ever get over my lost child, but at least I have someone to talk to now. He's about up to my chest and very thin. He has red hair and only a couple freckles. He has green eyes and says he has never left the state. Before we left the house in the dad's Jeep, I had Eddie tie up his friend and little sister while I drained some blood from Dad into a butter bowl, to help me maintain my center while on the road. I knew it would be nearly seven hours before we arrived in the next capital, and I didn't want to risk killing Eddie on the way. Since just having my fingers covered in blood kept me from lashing out, I figured it wouldn't hurt to try. I kept the bowl in the passenger seat and whenever I started to feel shaky or tense, I just reached my hand into it and wiggled my fingers around. Every once in a while, it didn't seem to be enough, so I brought the bowl to my face and inhaled deeply; I've noticed that the smell of blood takes a bit of the weight off my chest. Though that technique helped, it still wasn't as satisfying as *fresh* blood. I'm obviously designed to be this way; because there's no other reason blood would bring someone so much peace. I'm just glad I finally got over trying to get over it. I accept my mission and I accept my fate.

I kept trying to engage Eddie in conversation during our trip, but he seemed distant for some reason, so I eventually gave up and allowed him to have his silent time. There were a couple police traffic stops as we were trying to leave Minnesota, but with my smile and Eddie's presence, I was waved straight through all of them. Apparently, they are searching for some sort of mad man. I don't plan to take a break from killing, but I decided that it would be a good idea to have a little bit of father/son time with Eddie. He needed to know he was in good hands, and as long as he was with me, nothing bad would happen to him. We picked up some food and found an Amusement Park. I thought it would be exciting, judging by the advertisements, but it was just a small community thing. Nonetheless, I enjoyed my time with Eddie, eating under the gazebo. He was still in his Superman PJ's, so I couldn't convince him to go into the water. He kept asking when he would be allowed to go back home, and I told him he *was* home, just to forget about all of that now.

But, he would never forget his past as long as he kept the same name, so I tried to change it. He said that he liked his name. I guess I'll just have to find another way to help him forget. After we ate, I needed to find a place to sleep. We found a hotel down the street, but they didn't offer to let me pay with cash, even though I told Eddie we would have to sleep in the car. I bet the assholes don't even realize that they could have spared someone's life tonight if they would have just let us in. But no, I had to go with Plan B. In an attempt to train Eddie, I explained that we needed to find a house to take that had no signs of kids, security cameras, multiple cars, or dogs. I showed him how to look for blind spots, and how to do a quick witness scan. I also told him that sometimes we need a house with a garage to hide the previous victim's vehicle. He seemed very concerned that I was explaining all of this to him. I can tell that he is only doing what I tell him because he is scared. I feel like he will run away the first chance he gets.

We found a house on Ingals Avenue that fit all of the criteria I mentioned earlier. I noticed the house at first, but I waited to see if Eddie would spot it. It took a couple trips back and forth, but he finally pointed it out. It had a one car garage, a privacy fence and tall bushes close to the front windows. We parked in the driveway and I looked around for any signs of potential witnesses or cameras. I noticed the next door neighbor had a window facing us, but they had their thick blind pulled down. Eddie noticed a camera on another house adjacent to our house. However, it was on their front porch, aimed downward, so we weren't in sight. It was about 10 p.m. and I was concerned that we would be noticed before we got to the back door, because of the time. I didn't want to be caught walking toward the house, so we waited for about ten minutes to give any possible witness an opportunity to approach us while our hands were still clean. After we were clear, we got out and made our way to the back gate. We were out of sight and the gate was unlocked, so we crept in. We made a quick scan of the yard to look for toys before going in. No toys in sight, so we made our way to the porch.

I told Eddie to knock on the door and back up, so the owner would walk out. I figured I could just repeat the technique I used with Zach. What I didn't count on was his absolute refusal to cooperate with me. He just sat on the porch step whimpering about missing his mom. I had to sit down and have another talk with him. I told him if he didn't do as I said, we would just head back to his mom's and he could watch me cut off her head and put it in the oven. I told him that I would duct tape his eyes open so he would have to watch it burn through the oven window. He immediately stood up and walked over to knock on the door. I hated saying that stuff to the kid, because I think it will make it more difficult to gain his trust, but I guess it is better that he listens out of fear than not listening at all.

When he knocked, the back light came on shortly after. The owner cracked the door only as wide as her chain lock would let her. She asked the boy what he wanted and Eddie replied that he was lost. The owner told him to just sit on the porch and she would phone the police to come help him. I reacted by jumping out of cover and kicking the door through. The chain broke and the door slammed into the old woman's face, knocking her down. I grabbed Eddie by the arm and pulled him through the door and handed him the hatchet. I told him it was her or his mom and he began attacking the lady until she stopped moving. He cried the whole time he was doing it, but at least he did what he was told. I walked around the house, looking for any other residents, but there were no other people in the house. That explains why the old woman was so reluctant to open her door. We walked to the hallway garage door, so we could open the outside door and stash the Jeep, but it turns out the woman was a hoarder. There was no room in the garage for a vehicle. I didn't want to find another house having made it this far, so we quickly grabbed junk from the garage and threw them into the kitchen. Once we'd made enough room, Eddie and me went out and moved the Jeep in. Now we are in the clear, so we're going to make ourselves at home while we plan our next move.

June 10, 2014 (9:50 a.m.)   Bismarck, ND

N/A

Dear Diary, I'm not sure I'm doing the right thing anymore. I know I have been wronged by the world, but I don't know *how*. I cannot shake my temptations anymore, and I have given in completely. Listening to Eddie cry to himself all night has got me thinking that I'm doing the wrong thing. I woke up a few times, forgetting where I am, and whom I was with. I heard sniffling and ran to Zach, only for it to be Eddie. I keep thinking Zach is still alive, and that I was planning to stop until he was taken from me. I gave my hatchet to Eddie and told him to hide it somewhere in the garage so that I couldn't find it, because I wanted to stop this bullshit. I told him that I was sorry for what I have done to him and that all I want is to find my child again. I told them that if he helps me, I would take him back home. He agreed, and we discussed ways in which we could track Abram down. Eddie said we should go back to his home, but unfortunately I cannot backtrack. Everywhere I go; people are trying to hunt me down.

We decided to just sit around for the day and watch the news, hoping to hear that Heather has been found. I was on almost all of the news channels, but there was no sign of Heather. Maybe I'll just give up on her. I know she probably has a mouthful of maggots by now. Eddie has been chipper all morning, since he feels that he will be going back home. However, even while I write this, I'm already getting the itch, and I'm probably not going to be taking him back. I need him to get into houses and to gain people's trust. I just need to figure out how to disguise him. He has too many male features to turn him into a girl so I'll just shave his head. I still can't see Zach's face.

June 10, 2014 (2:40 p.m.)   Bismarck, ND

Eddie (60)

Holy fuck, Diary! What kind of animal am I? I don't know what to do anymore. I just need to kill myself before any more kids get hurt. I know one thing for sure; I'm never taking another child with me again. I can't stop shaking and my ears are ringing louder than ever. I had to burn my book bag with everything in it except for you, my gun, and my ammo. Now I need to find more clothes and money. Why the hell did I keep the money in the bag? It's because it was in the same pocket as the hair and clothes. I am having a little trouble breathing, but I am not reacting as bad as I did when it was Zach that I lost. I don't think anything could ever bother me that badly again.

Damn it all to hell. I was shaving Eddie's hair with some clippers I found in a hoarder box. We were laughing and telling jokes. He was excited to help me find Abram and go home to his mom. I wasn't ready to tell him that I had changed my mind. My plan was to keep him thinking it until he forgot. The problem is that I completely forgot about my reaction to seeing Heather's hair in the bottom of my bag. I collected all of Eddie's hair to keep it, and when I saw *her* hair, I felt my chest sink and my body getting hot. When I looked up, Eddie was gone. I didn't know where he went or when he left. I figured I just had some kind of time lapse, until I noticed that the bathroom mirror and window were both busted. I began to panic, and ran throughout the house yelling for Eddie.

He was sitting straight up on the living room couch and his head was missing. I began to vomit, and I sat at his feet weeping for a couple hours. I didn't go into my dark cave, but it still affected me greatly. I didn't feel like I lost my child, but I *knew* that I was the one who did it. I knew that I was the animal that hurt this child. I probably would have ended up taking him home at some point if he refused to forget. But that's all out the window now. What the fuck is with the headless body on the couch technique? How the hell do I end up in the same place I started? It's like I look in my bag, and then I look up. How am I still in that position when I regain consciousness? I searched the house for Eddie's head. It was in the kitchen sink with knife handles sticking out both eye sockets and a smile carved from ear to chin to ear. As soon as I realized what I was looking at, I puked all over his face. What the hell is wrong with me, Diary? Is this happening because of Zach's memory, or because my journey is starting to impact my mind? It could just be the combination of the two. Regardless of *why*, I understand how it happens. I decided to never look in that bag again. After seeing Eddie's head, I immediately set fire to my bag and set it the bathtub. This should never happen again. But if it does, perhaps I will end it all. I don't have any idea what to do from here. I don't know if I can ever feel good again. Fuck it, I'm going to sleep. Maybe this will go away.

June 11, 2014 (11:00 p.m.)   Bismarck, ND

N/A

Dear Diary, I think it will be ok now. I have rediscovered my sanity. I have spent the day reading some of my passages, and I'm actually embarrassed a little at how cowardly and emotional I have become. I can't let myself feel again or I'll screw up and end up getting caught. I laid for most of the day yesterday just whimpering and feeling down. It's like the whole world was on fire. Just before I dozed off, I heard a knock at the door. I grabbed my gun and rushed toward it. I just *knew* it was the police, but I was wrong. When I peered through the door, I noticed two Mormons trying to sell me some kind of bullshit. After everything I've been through, my faith has gone. I contemplated ignoring them so they would go away, but I decided that I would kill them instead. I mean, I felt like shit, so whatever. Before letting them in, I'll ask who they are, because I'm tired of killing faceless humans. I need to know them. I need to know they are real. They identified themselves as John and Chase from the Mormon Church; hear to spread the good word. So I opened the door and allowed them in. Their first expressions were of slight shock since I was still covered in blood. I told them not to be alarmed because I'm a novice chef that just had a fight with a bottle of meatloaf sauce. John is about my height and chunkier than I am. He has short, brown hair that he keeps greased back. Chase, on the other hand is about four inches shorter than me with a shaved head and a weird little mustache. I can't stop looking at that mustache.

They began to giggle a little as they walked through the door. The couch with Eddie's body was to my left, so I walked backward and to the right. They followed me, while maintaining eye contact and not noticing the grizzly scene behind them. They went on to promote their religious team and explain why it was the correct one. I kept nodding my head and showing interest, while I considered what to do with them. I knew that if I killed them with the gun, it would attract the neighbors and I wouldn't enjoy it all that much. I also knew that if I killed them both at the same time, it would be a waste. While they were asking me if I'd like to visit their church, I started to realize that I needed to try something new. I felt horrible for what I did to Eddie and I needed to find a way to make myself forget. I decided I would keep them and experiment on them for a couple days before ending them.

At this time I had my gun in the back of my pants, so I reached behind and pulled it to reveal to the Mormons what a bad idea it was to talk to strangers. I aimed it at them and told them to get on their knees. They were crying, praying, and asking me to spare them. Now, this confused the shit out of me because only seconds prior to that moment, they were bragging about how cool death was. I asked if they were armed, or if they had phones or wallets. Neither was armed but both had phones and wallets with a decent bit of money in them.

"Just take the money and let us go."

"Oh, I will, just be patient." Luckily for me, I remember that I threw a pack of large plastic zip ties in the kitchen. I told them to get on their bellies and close their eyes if they wanted to live. I then quickly went around the corner to grab the zip ties. When I came back, they were right where I left them. I restrained their hands behind their backs and tied their legs together. When I rolled John over, he noticed Eddie on the couch and started to scream. I put the gun barrel in his mouth and started slowly sliding it down his throat until he began expelling his last meal. Afterward, they were both quiet with the exception of that continuous sobbing and praying. I actually think I overheard one of them asking God to kill me. I didn't realize that was something you could pray for. Apparently I'm behind on the rules.

I found some old dog chain in the pile of crap in the kitchen, and I used it to tie them to the hot water tank which resided in a small closet area in the back wall of the living room. My logic was that if they tried too hard to get loose, the tank would fall and perhaps burn them enough to scream for me. I carried Eddie and his head out back and buried him under a cherry tree. I then removed Chase from his restraints long enough to walk out and say some words for Eddie's burial.

June 12, 2014 (6:30 p.m.)   Bismarck, ND

N/A

Dear Diary, my experiments started today. I think torture is almost as enjoyable as death itself, with the added benefit that I get to keep my fix on tap. I cut all of the clothes off both men and I laid them on the living room floor, facing each other's feet. I found some thicker gauged wire in the kitchen that I used to tie their legs together in several locations, to reduce *flopability*. I then moved them close and tied them together in more than a dozen locations. They were restrained tight and Chase's toes were at Jason's mouth while Jason's ankles were at Chase's mouth. I dumped some steak sauce on their feet and told them that this would be their next meal. You should have seen their reactions to the news. I guess they believed me when I told them I would let them go if they cooperated. It looked like a giant ham wrapped in twine, franticly wiggling and screaming. I had to remove one ear each to let them know that screaming was not a good thing to do.

June 13, 2014 (7:40 p.m.)   Bismarck, ND

N/A

Dear Diary, nobody has eaten yet. I spent the whole evening yesterday eating and watching the show. I hoped they would at least take a taste or something. They were successful in figuring out how to work as a team to roll from one side of the room to the other. I can't really figure out how I feel about this though. I have never watched anyone this long. My emotions go up and down almost constantly, so they must think something is wrong with me by now. One moment I would be trying to find things to dump on them, and the next I was considering letting them go. I don't know what to do from one minute to the other. The only thing I do know is that ever since I stained their faces with ear blood, I haven't been anxious or sad. I have forgotten about Eddie for the most part, but Zach keeps popping in my head. I don't know if I'll ever be able to get over that. I haven't had a knock on the door or a phone call since I've been here, so I'm thinking that the home owner wasn't very popular. I did end up going back to her body to remove some toes though. I thought that maybe if I primed their stomachs, they would begin eating. I forced a toe in each of the Mormons' mouths at gun point and told them to chew. They chewed all they could but ended up spitting the toes out after a while. I should have known that they wouldn't be able to chew up bone. I ensured them that when they are hungry enough to begin eating each other's feet, they could eat around the bone.

June 13, 2014 (10:25 p.m.)   Bismarck, ND

Jason & Chase (62)

Dear Diary, there is human shit all over the house, and I don't think I can stay much longer. I had to speed things up a little because they were still refusing to eat. I found some wire cutters and started cutting off fingers until they started eating. I only had to remove two from Jason before he started eating Chase's foot. Chase was screaming, so had to tie a towel around his throat – just tight enough to reduce the volume without completely blocking his air. I told him that his friend was going to town so he might as well fall in. He tried to refuse, until I pulled out the cutters. He then began chowing down on Jason's ankle and the blood began flowing. I seized the moment and brought my face down to his and rubbed the blood around on his face while staring into his eyes. He was taking bigger bites each time. I think they were actually fighting in a way. I stepped back and watched as they attempted to devour each other. I couldn't handle the smell of shit anymore so I strangled each one of them by hand. Oh my God, the whole experience was *wonderful*, well, beside the shit smell. I felt quenched and rejuvenated as I sat there on my knees admiring the art I had created. My body began to feel weak, so I lay across them like a puppy and fell asleep. I haven't felt that relaxed since Benjamin. I just woke up a little bit ago, and I'm thinking probably going to pick up my mission where I left off.

June 14, 2014 (6:20 p.m.)   Bismarck, ND

N/A

Dear Diary, I'm going to need to make a judgment call about something and I'm not sure exactly how to feel about it. Well, I was feeling amazing yesterday, after having my craving fully satisfied. I decided to pocket the $430 that I got from those Mormon wallets. I'm not sure why they would be carrying that much cash, but who am I to complain? I thought I deserved to treat myself to some pizza after all I have been through. While I pondered on what to have on my pizza, I shaved and took a shower. Luckily for me, Jason's clothes were a near-perfect fit. I now have a white button up shirt with black dress pants and shiny black shoes. I feel like a new man. I decided I wanted pepperoni, mushrooms, and banana peppers on a thick crust. I placed the call from the house phone and watched some cartoons while I waited. About ten minutes before the pizza arrived, I realized that the house smelled like shit and there were bodies everywhere. I just wanted to eat my pizza in peace without the delivery guy standing in the way. If he saw the bodies, I would have to kill him as well. Also, I'm sure he's being timed on his delivery and the pizza company knows exactly where he is. I wondered if it would be better to wait out front with the money so he wouldn't see anything. But, he would see me and I know this house will be on the news soon. Up till this point, the only witnesses have been children, and from the police sketch I saw on the news, they were so scared that their imaginations went wild. I look nothing like the big, crazy man that people believe is me.

I decided to just force the pizza guy to call work and quit so they wouldn't be waiting for him. I would then eat the pizza and kill the guy or probably kill the guy first, then eat the pizza. It doesn't matter; I just knew I would take his car and drive it to the next state. However, it didn't work out as planned. When he arrived, I met him outside the front door. He had long hair, a nose ring, and tattoo sleeves. I found out later that his name is Brandon. I handed him the money and while he counted the change, I asked him to step in so my cat wouldn't get out. He stepped in while still counting the money. When he looked up to see where the smell was coming from, he noticed the scene and when he turned to me, he was welcomed with the barrel of my gun. My plan would have worked perfectly, but instead of screaming like everyone else, Brandon didn't seem bothered at all. He just handed me my change and asked how I could eat my pizza with that stench. I directed him to sit on one end of the couch while I sat at the other end, trying to wrap my mind around his behavior. I didn't waste any time breaking into the pizza though. He sat back calmly and began watching the cartoon that was on and asked me if I wouldn't mind if he had a piece to eat.

Bewildered, I sat there with the gun on my lap, eating dinner with a stranger. I asked him why he wasn't scared and he told me that he will die one day anyway, so why not today? He also said that pizza is the perfect last meal. I just finished eating and I decided to write everything down while I planned my next move. Do I kill him? Do I let him go? He knows my identity, but doesn't seem concerned. Do I take him with me? He's an adult and I already know I can't trust an adult. He is still eating very slowly, and he has actually laughed on two separate instances at the TV. How could someone be so relaxed? He's the exact opposite of me; he is who I wish I could be. I'm not sure what to do, so I'll give it some thought before making any kind of real decision.

June 15, 2014 (10:11 p.m.)   Pierre, SD

N/A

Dear Diary, I decided to give Brandon a chance. Last night I told him that I couldn't let him go, but I didn't want to kill him either. I asked him what he thought I should do. He asked me why not just let him join me on my journey. I asked him how he knows about my journey. He responded with, "Dude, you're obviously the Traveler that everyone has been talking about." My stomach sank, but he said he had a totally different idea about what I looked like. I asked him to call his work before it got too late and quit his job and then I would consider it. He did as I asked and didn't even try to tell on me. He told me he was one of my biggest fans. I was astounded by the statement, because I didn't understand how anyone could like me for what I do – but it made me feel pretty good to hear it. I asked him about his background and found that he was a horror junky that was obsessed with serial killers and he played drums for a hardcore metal band. I haven't really listened to a whole lot of that screaming music, but I've never gave it a chance either. Could that be the secret to his level of comfort?

Brandon lives alone in a studio apartment and his girlfriend just left him last week. I guess his suicidal antics make sense to me now. He said he has never killed anyone, but he has thought about it a lot. I retrieved my hatchet from Eddie's lame hiding spot in the garage and handed it to him, while directing him to try it on the big ham in the middle of the floor. I wanted him to tell me how it makes him feel. He hesitated at first and I thought he may have just been a good liar, trying to get the best of me. But once he started chopping away at the dead Mormons, he didn't stop until he was completely exhausted. He lowered himself to the floor and leaned back on the couch with his eyes nearly rolled into the back of his head. He told me that it was the most amazing feeling he has ever felt. I think I might have my first actual friend, but we needed to set the scene to clear his name before we left town. I asked him to give me his work shirt and he did. It's a good thing he had another one under it because the only male clothes around were all cut up. I stabbed a hole through the front of his work shirt and told Brandon to cut his arm, allowing it bleed on the evidence. He did as I asked, and I put the shirt on top of the pizza box. It seemed like I might have stabbed him and done something with his body.

We spent the night driving to end up here in Pierre. We are parked alongside the Missouri River and discussed what our next move would be. He asked about my Diary, and I told him it is private. He is nineteen years old and anxious to learn from me.

June 16, 2014 (11:15 a.m.)   Pierre, SD

Brandon (63)

Dear Diary, Brandon liked to talk a whole lot and he chewed much too loudly. After spending the night driving around the city, I began to realize that I'm not meant to have friends. Every time my mind started to settle, I would hear him again. I miss Zach and I cannot replace him. I have already settled with that. I thought I would be able to learn from Brandon since he seemed to be at peace with himself, but the more he talked, the more I realized how *much* he actually talks. As he rambled, I began scratching my jeans and tried to stay focused on the relaxing sound that makes. I finally had to ask him to remain silent for a while. He did as I asked, so I began thinking that maybe I could have friends after all, as long as he would obey me whenever I made a demand. It was quiet for several minutes, until a yellow cat wearing a wizard hat jumped on the hood of the car. It caught me off guard but, since it was all dressed up, I figured the owner had to be close. I told Brandon that we needed to be going because someone was sure to be looking for their cat.

Brandon giggled a little and then said, "What cat, man?" I pointed it out to him, thinking that he must be about blind. He sat up and stared out the window. The cat put its nose to the window and stared straight into his face. Brandon turned to me and told me that he didn't see anything. What the hell Diary? Am I starting to see things, or what? Well, the cat looked back to me, and we locked gazes for about ten minutes. He then said in a deep, movie trailer voice, "Just kill him already." I nearly shat my pants as I looked at Brandon to double check that he wasn't seeing the same thing. My heart started to race and inside my head was sounding like someone was turning the volume up and down on a guitar amp. When I looked back, the cat was gone, and I let out a sigh of relief. Just then, I noticed the dumb little wizard cat was sitting on my lap, looking up at me. I was afraid to move. He then said, "Dude, I'm hungry, just kill him already." I was in the middle of what seemed to be a panic attack, so I did as the cat commanded. I grabbed my gun from beside the seat and shot Brandon in the back of the head just as he was looking out his window. The thought of bystanders didn't even occur to me. I just watched as the cat smiled at me as it casually climbed up to sit on Brandon's shoulder. He then began eating pieces of brain fragments that were sliding down the pizza man's neck.

I couldn't turn away, but then he said, "Good job, dork." and disappeared. What the hell did he mean by *dork*? What did I do to make him think I was a dork? One thing is for sure, he must be a sorcerer. Cats are weird though, so, oh well. Maybe *he* will be my friend? Perhaps he could do spells or something? It would be awesome if the cat could turn me invisible. Then I could just kill people all day and no one would know how it was happening. That would be nice.

June 17, 2014 (1:40 a.m.)   Pierre, SD

Mom and Dad (65)

Dear Diary, I found a little yellow house on Capital Avenue that I thought would be a perfect place to spend the night. However, when I began to walk around to the back door, I heard some voices on the back porch. It was weird because they were talking like pirates, saying "R" after everything. I thought it may be people getting ready for a play or something, but nonetheless, there were too many for me to take over. I hid in a bush beside the house to wait until everyone left. I waited for about an hour or so, but I didn't see anyone leave. I did a double check of the driveway and there was only one car. I figured they must have already left, without me noticing, so I decided to try again. As I walked toward the back yard, I heard the pirates again. I continued to the back yard until I noticed my feet were wet. I looked down and I was standing in water up to my ankles. My heart started racing and I looked around the corner of the house. The whole yard was water with a perimeter of thick fog. There were two women and a man sitting in a little wooden sailboat beside the back door. I didn't know why someone would fill their back yard with water, but who am I to judge?

My plan was to walk along the house until I got to the people, and then show them my gun for entry into their house. The problem is, that the closer I got, the more I could tell that they were *real* pirates. They were dressed the part, and their sail had a big white skull on it. It was too weird for me, so I decided to try another house. When I reached the sidewalk, the stupid cat showed up again. I asked it what it wanted, and he said, "Nothin' but food, dude. Where are we going to get some food?" I told him that from what I can recall, he just ate. I thought it was gross that he ate people – but to each his own. We kept walking until we reached a bigger grey house with a brown door, all windows open, and only one car. The cat said, "Hey, I bet they taste good." I couldn't relate, but I did agree that it looked like a good target. I walked around the side of the house, toward the back yard, and there was nothing there out of the ordinary. I looked down and the cat was gone again. Instead of knocking on the back door, I decided to just go through the open kitchen window. I climbed on top of the air conditioning unit and pulled my way into the house. I remained hidden behind the blue curtains as I listened to the sounds of the house. Someone was in the middle of cooking a meal, because the oven was on and there were various foods and spices lying around. When I knew the coast was clear, I came out from behind the blinds, grabbed a knife from the drawer, and crawled toward the kitchen entry way. They had a double door – like an old saloon – between the kitchen and dining room, so I peered from below.

I noticed a family of three sitting at a table, playing cards. It was an older man and woman, with a teenage boy. The boy looked old enough to kill, so I wasn't concerned. I scanned the room and noticed they had an alarm panel on the wall by the front door, but how good is that if they leave their windows open? Freak'n idiots deserve to be slaughtered. I stayed huddled beside the refrigerator while I tried to come up with a stealthy plan. It would be unpredictable if I decided to just run in slashing. I was taking too long to come up with something, so I had to find a place to hide while I thought things through. Their kitchen has a pantry near the back door. I crawled to the door and quietly let myself in. My brain was fried, and I couldn't seem to process anything. While I was sitting in the dark pantry, I heard the mother in the kitchen preparing plates. I considered taking her out, and then it would only be the father and son. I didn't do it though. By the time I cracked the door to come out, she was already eating with the family. I sat a while longer until I heard someone in the kitchen cleaning up.

I heard the back door open and a dog came into the house. I felt like I was going to get caught when I saw the dog's nose under the pantry door. He must have smelled the cat on me. I pulled out the gun because there's no way I was going to take out a dog and a family of three with just a knife. I knew that when I opened fire, I wouldn't be able to spend the night, but I didn't believe I had another choice. I heard the boy say, "Stop being dumb, boy." I thought they would check to see what the dog was sniffing at, but they didn't. I had to get him away from the door, so grabbed a hand full of spaghetti noodles from a box on a shelf. I then rammed them quickly up the dog's nose to send him yelping into the other room. I kept my gun handy, just in case the family wondered what had happened. Again, no one was checking the pantry. After a while, I heard the television and all of their voices in the other room. I must have been very tired, because I dozed off in the corner on a pile of towels and rags. When I woke up, the house was silent and I didn't know what time it was. I crept out, and the only light was a dim wall light in the hallway between the living room and bedrooms. I knew that the dog was somewhere, and I didn't want to alarm him. While I made my way to the parents' room, I saw the dog sleeping on the bathroom floor. I had to take him out first, so I quietly crawled up to his side. He was an older Golden Retriever, so he was bound to go soon anyway. In one motion, I held his mouth shut and started rapidly stabbing him in the shoulder region, hoping to hit his heart. It didn't make much noise, so I was good to go with the rest of the family. I continued to crawl down the hall and the first room I came to was the boy's room. As I got closer, I heard some quiet moaning and a faint sound of crying. I was startled, because I thought everyone was asleep. When I peeked in through the door, I was astounded by what I witnessed.

The dad was on the boy's bed and both were naked. The boy was giving the dad oral, which made me throw up in my mouth a little. I know I'd planned to kill the boy, but that desire left me quickly – and now I felt that he actually needed protection. I passed by the room to take out the mother first. I came to the mother's room and she was sound asleep, oblivious to what happens in her house at night. I wanted to show her before she died, so I held her mouth shut and tapped her head with the gun. She woke up and went stiff. I whispered in her ear that there was something she needed to see, but I needed her to be quiet. She nodded her head and I guided her to the boy's room. When she saw what was going on, she screamed hysterically. She seemed to have forgotten I was even there. The dad pushed the boy's head away from his genitals and covered himself up. He couldn't formulate an excuse, so the only thing that escaped from his mouth was, "What the fuck are you doing up?" She lunged at him and started attacking him as he lay there on his back, kicking up like a little bitch. I walked up behind them and moved her aside. I told her I would take care of it. I shoved the knife through the center of the father's neck. He began to flop around, making loud bubbling sounds as his life slowly ended. While this was going on, the woman directed her attention to me and tried to attack me, too. It's like she'd forgotten what she had just witnessed. I punched her in the side of the head, knocking her unconscious.

The boy of about 14 was lying naked on his bed with his face in his pillow. He cried out loud, telling me to leave him alone, and that he hadn't seen my face. I thought again about the option to spare him or not. I didn't know how well he could identify me. I also wondered if I would be doing him a favor by killing him, after everything he has gone through. It's not like he would be able to live a normal life or anything. Besides, they say that a molester is created by being molested, so perhaps I would be killing a future molester? And, how could I let him live when he was old enough to really identify me? But, how could I end his life if it wouldn't make me feel better? I told him to keep his head down while I thought about it. He just kept crying and swearing that he didn't see anything. I never started out to be an animal; I'm not a fan of who I have become, and if I killed a boy who has obviously been abused most of his life, I'm not sure how I would feel about myself. I realize that emotions are fairly new to me, but I can't just ignore them.

I sat at the foot of the bed, hoping that I could just figure out what to do, but nothing would push through. What is wrong with me, Diary? I don't know why my mind is slowing down so much. I used to be quick on my feet, but now I just can't seem to decide on anything. The bed sheets were blue and there was a wooden rocking chair by the window. Why would a boy need a rocking chair? While I was attempting to process some rational thoughts, the mother started to squirm around on the floor as she slowly woke up. I couldn't determine how I felt about the boy's life, but the mother's was all too easy. I grabbed a video game controller from the small entertainment center that rested along the wall beyond the foot of the bed. I wrapped its wire around both of my hands about three times, and then mounted her back. She wasn't all the way awake yet, so when she felt her air passages collapsing, she just gave up. I think she was done with life anyway. She initially reached behind to grab my forearm, but let go well before she was dead. She just went limp and I could almost feel her shoulders shrug, like she was saying, "Whatever."

The boy was crying louder, now that he had the rational assumption that his mom was dead. But, to my surprise, his face was still buried under his pillow like he'd been told. While I sat there pondering, the thoughts of Zach's kidnapping and the unfortunate death of Eddie rolled around in my head. I immediately realized that this boy was still just a boy and that if I killed him, I would probably feel sad. I don't like feeling sad.

June 17, 2014 (3:25 p .m.)   Pierre, SD

Dear Diary, last night I decided to let Tony live. We talked for a while, but he never looked at my face. Apparently, he was adopted and has only been living with his family for two years. The father started messing around with him after the first couple weeks. He didn't want to say anything, in the fear of being sent back into foster care. I thought he could be the perfect partner, but then I remembered Eddie again and decided against it. I can't have a companion on my journey, because I'm too unstable. I don't even know what I'm going to do before I do it. I really feel like killing everyone, but then after someone is bleeding below me, I sometimes begin to regret it. I used to love the sensation of watching someone perish, but now I am really starting to not enjoy it much. I don't make sense anymore. Who am I? I am not defined as a person – or an animal. When I was strangling the adoptive mother, I wasn't *thinking*. My body was on some kind of autopilot, and all I could think about was the desire to kill. For that brief moment, there were no other thoughts in my head. All of my concerns and worries just flew right out my ear. I am used to that, but I didn't need to do it, and I didn't really want to until I saw her moving. After she was dead, I started feeling horrible again. I don't know. Maybe by explaining my emotions, I can attempt to take control of them?

Before I see the victim, my head is full of everything. I can't seem to get a moment away from my constant reflections. When I begin to plan an attack, it's the only thing on my mind. This is better than having a thousand things going on at once. It is peaceful. When the person is struggling or suffering, I feel energized and excited. I am separated from my body, and everything seems perfect. The ending is what confuses me the most. I used to keep that bit of peace for a while, and there was no such thing as regret. Now, the end is weird. It can only be compared to being really horny and having sex with a prostitute. It seems like the right thing to do, until you're done with the act and you're left staring into the eyes of a soulless vessel. You are worse off than when you began. When the victim is gone, there is no amount of regret that can bring them back. Did I really *need* to kill that woman? What did it do for me? Why can't I get a grip…Oh well, fuck it. I've been out this long. There's no reason to stop now.

Anyway, I used his video game cords to tie up the kid's feet and hands. I promised him I would leave today if he just stayed in bed and didn't do anything funny. I finished their leftovers and watched some television. While I've been sitting around writing this, I just watched a news lady rant about me for a while, after showing the scene where they discovered Brandon's body. They showed a map of all of my murder locations, which showed a red line of my travels. I was spooked, because they were talking about road blocks everywhere, curfews, arming yourself, and all kinds of other precautions to prevent me from hurting anyone else. They still don't have a good sketch of me yet, so I'm not too concerned. I'm just going to have to start mixing it up a little, because I'm obviously becoming predictable. All of the bordering states of South Dakota are on some kind of high alert while they wait for me to stop for a visit. Well, I won't be doing that now, will I?

June 17, 2014 (4:36 p .m.)   Pierre, SD

Hell yeah, Diary, I'm *alive* again!! I was fucking off and watching some shitty reality show and there was a breaking news story–Heather has been found!! Alive!! She showed up in Bowling Green, Kentucky at a gas station. She looked slightly beaten and dead in the eyes, but she was *alive*. They didn't show her talking, but they showed her getting out of a cop car and being escorted into a hospital. My life suddenly had meaning again. But, while I was trying to figure out how to go get her, the news was talking about how she had identified the *"Traveler."* My stomach sunk, not for the thought of being caught, but for the thought of betrayal. That was, until they reported that she had killed him. She was protecting me, Diary. She told the cops that Abram kidnapped her and killed her parents. She described everything we did together, but she put Abram in my place. She described herself as a scared hostage who had to perform sexual acts on him. That's all they had covered of her side of the story, but with all of my joy, I began to become enraged. My God, I am sorry for everything I have done. I hate myself for it, and I promise to try harder to quit. Please just get me back my child.

Also, God, what the fuck is with all of these people wanting to fuck kids? Why did this become a thing? It doesn't make sense. There are tons of desperate women out there with full-sized dick tunnels all ready for action. *What the fuck?* I am just now starting to see it for some reason. Was I blind until someone did it to my child? The guy in Michigan attempted to rape Heather when she was Zach, then this guy in the back room, *then* Abram. Why is this just now starting to bother me? Why is *something* bothering me? ,I kind of like having someone to hate for a good reason, so I'm just going to go with it. I'm going to get Heather back if it's the last thing I do. Oh shit, Diary, that boy is still tied up back there. I need to be going, so he can eat. But wait, if his family is found like this, wouldn't it mess up Heather's story? I can't let her be seen as a liar. Damn. *Damn!* Why couldn't I have waited a while longer to kill someone?

June 17, 2014 (9:50 p.m.)   Pierre, SD

Tony (66)

Dear Diary, I'm sorry but I had to do it. I had no choice. If I would have let him live, he would have been able to alert the police and allow them to see a big hole in the timeline. Abram could have killed Brandon and then driven straight to Kentucky. Hopefully Heather doesn't talk any more than she has to and allow the cops to rule out that possibility. I'm not going to discuss how I killed Tony, because I am not proud of it; it did me no satisfaction, and I didn't learn anything from it. I just need to have a good couple days before the bodies are found. I don't need any witness saying "yesterday" or "this morning." I'm packing up everything I can here, and I'm heading to Kentucky to get her back. Since she is telling a story to protect me, I'm sure she will come with me.

June 18, 2014 (10:40 p.m.)   Kansas City, KS

N/A

Dear Diary, I have traveled for what seems to be forever on I-29. I ended up just taking the family car rather than trying to kill anyone else. The border stops haven't been as thorough as the news had mentioned – In fact, I didn't get stopped once. There does seem to be a lot of people getting pulled over, though. I just need to continue driving sober. Anyway, I found a house on Bales Ave that looked abandoned. I just waited until I knew there were no witnesses, and then drove around to the back yard. I just need a place to spend the night. The level of excitement I have been experiencing since the update about Zach has drained me physically. I do have to admit, this house is a bit freaky. It is made of brick and all of the windows are black, plastic trash bags. The back porch is pretty much nonexistent, with a sunken roof and rotted supports.

The moon reminds me of something you'd see on a werewolf movie. I thought about going inside the house, but I decided I would rather live to see another day. Hmm, I wonder if I'm going crazy. I know that cat had to be imagined, and the more I think about it, pirates don't live in fucking South Dakota…

What if I'd imagined the news story about Zach as well? That is depressing to consider. I have been worked up over it all night and day. If it turns out to be a mind trick, I'm probably just going to end it, because there's no way I can lose my kid twice. Nah, it had to be real. Right? What is *real*? I think the thought of starting a family again is making my cravings go away. I haven't thought of killing someone since yesterday. Please let this be true.

What is my plan? I haven't really thought this through very well. Heather has a story that I need to help her maintain. If someone finds this car and realizes how far it is from the owner's body, they will know her tale is false. I'm so stupid. Why can't I think anymore? When was my last shower? Am I hungry? I've definitely fallen into my own reality, haven't I? Reading through my Diary, I don't even know if I have a son or daughter. I know it was Heather, and Zach was just a cover, but Zach grew on me as my son. It would be weird to have a daughter. I know she is the same person, though. I guess it would be better to let her just go back to being Heather. But when I get her, I can't allow her keep that identity. Am I going to break in wherever she is and take her again? How's this going to work? How hard will she be to find? I wonder how she killed Abram. I know she loves me, because she never killed me, even though she had several chances. I don't know. Maybe I'll just wing it. Why not? Wait…What the hell was that? Dude, there's a fucking face in the upstairs window of this house. The hell with this, I'm out of here.

June 19, 2014 (2:15 a.m.)   Kansas City, KS

Homeless Man (67)

Dear Diary, I couldn't leave. As I started to pull out, I saw a cop parked down the street, along the road. I quickly reversed back into my hiding spot. There was a small fire flickering from the upstairs window, and I kept seeing a face. I thought my chances were better facing a demon than pulling out in front of a cop. Initially, I considered just running through the back yards to escape, but if it wasn't a ghost in there, I'd have a witness to worry about. There was no other way in, except the cellar door, beside what was left of the porch. I thought I would be frightened, because it just seemed like I should be. However, as I descended the pitch black steps, glazing my body in spider webs, I realized that I didn't experience fear anymore. It felt good to be myself again. That is the only downfall of having a child. She gave me a reason to feel emotions and worry about my existence. It seems that I've been away from her long enough to lose all of those feelings. As I reached the bottom of the steps, and began dragging my feet, with my arms up as a barrier to avoid head injury, I wondered if I even wanted to have that back in my life at all. She has turned me into a crybaby little bitch.

As I climbed the steps into what appeared to be the kitchen area, I realized that the time I'd spent with Heather was the best time of my life. She may have turned me into a bitch, but I was happy around her. When I got to the top of the second flight of stairs, I saw the light at the end of the hall and smelled burnt clothing. I tiptoed like a cartoon character to the doorway that concealed the light. The door was gone, though. Perhaps it is lost somewhere in the house. Maybe it would be fun to track it down. Anyway, I peeked around, and witnessed a bald, homeless guy with a jean jacket and black sweat pants. He was lying on a pile of assorted clothes and blankets. He had created a nest, and beside him was what appeared to be a whole grocery sack full of lighters. He was on his side, and in a metal coffee can was a small fire. I knew it was a sock he was burning, because the toe of it was hanging out of the can.

I thought he was asleep, so I tried to sneak up on him to kill him in his sleep. At this point, all I had was my book bag. I don't remember where my weapons are. I've either left them in the car, or at the last house, but I figured I could take out one guy simply by choking him. What I didn't consider was the floor's integrity, and the fact that the guy was just looking at me through the window a couple minutes ago. I should have known he wasn't asleep. Well, I was about half-way between him and the doorway when my foot fell through some rotted flooring. Just then, he jumped up like some kind of wild-eyed ape with blackened teeth. He ran at me, wielding a kitchen knife. Luckily for me, both of his feet fell through the flooring about 2 feet further away than arm's reach. I was stuck at my knee, trying to pull free, but my pants were caught on a nail or something. He was stuck at his hips, screaming at me in some kind of meth language, while still trying to stab me. He just kept on scratching and stabbing at the floor, as if hoping it would let him go. I took a minute to observe the situation. It almost seemed like he thought he was being eaten by a shark, and that if he injured it bad enough, he could get free. The more he became aware of how stuck he was, the more he totally freaked out.

I eventually wiggled free and walked slowly around the perimeter of the room, trying to avoid the crazy little slasher-man. I thought the cop may hear him if he got any louder, so I needed a way to shut him up. I found a piece of 2x4 that was about 3-feet long, lying under the window. I walked slowly up to the man and hit his knife hand as hard as I could with the board, and his weapon slid away, across the floor. His face changed as he stared up at me holding a piece of lumber. It is like he finally realized that this would be his last day. I wanted to tie his mouth shut, but I didn't trust his arms. I hit him in the shoulders and arms until I was able to deem them inoperable. I then grabbed a t-shirt and wrapped it around his face to reduce him to a mute. I didn't know if he had alarmed anyone or not, so I sat there for a while before making my next move. I would rather be caught with a beat-up bum than a dead one. Once I was comfortable that we were still alone, I began to consider my plans for him.

I suddenly began to wonder what I was even doing here. Heather is out there alive, and I'm not supposed to be making a blood trail to her. But, here I am again. I wasn't even thinking about the end game. What sucked is that I knew I was too deep into this one to back out. I needed to find a way to get rid of the car *and* to eliminate this guy without it looking like I'd done it. I wanted to mix it up. Then, I heard a knock on the window. This startled me, because I was two stories up. I went to the window to check it out, and sure enough, it was the cat again. This time he had a clown hat on, and his little nose was blue. I couldn't help but to let out a little giggle as I opened the window to allow him to float in. I asked him what he wanted. He said, "Dude's not dead, food is what I said. Hand me that lighter and I'll make his day a little brighter." I did as the cat said, and handed him a lighter from the grocery sack. As I watched him use it, I realized that he had little human thumbs. This tripped me out. He had his claws out, gripping the lighter, but the little thumb poked right out the top of his paw. "What he fuck, man? You have thumbs?" He said, "Well, yeah." He floated over to the bum, who started to panic once more. I could swear that he saw the cat, too, so maybe I'm not crazy after all. Maybe it is one of God's angels sent here to help me with my journey.

He pulled the man's hair backwards with one paw and held the lighter flame right under his Adam's apple. The smells and sounds were atrocious. He held the flame in place for several minutes. The bum's skin was boiling, turning black, and seemed to melt away from his throat. The blood was running down his neck after a while. The flame finally made its way to his esophagus. Once that was penetrated, the cat had a hard time keeping the lighter ignited. It was a fairly small hole, but there were some high pitch whistling escaping from it. Mr. Bum wouldn't die, though. After the hole was big enough, the cat slid the lighter down to block the air flow. There was some rapid tossing and gargling but the guy finally ended up dying. The cat then started eating the bum's ears while purring. Then, he suddenly vanished and I was staring down at the guy's face with his hair pulled back in my left hand. As for my right hand, I had blood running down my wrist, and a couple blisters on my thumb. I jumped back and crab walked to the wall. Was that me? Am I the cat or did he magically *poof* me there after he'd disappeared?

June 23, 2014 (11:45 p.m.)   Bowling Green, KY

Old Man (68)

Dear Diary, I can feel the energy rising because I know I'm getting closer to her. Oh, I bet you're wondering about how I got here. No time for that, though. It has been four days since my last entry. When I arrived, I tried to avoid killing anyone, but it didn't work very well. There are more police around here than I have ever seen. I have even seen a couple military trucks drive down the street. I'm not sure what is going on around here, but I feel it has something to do with Heather. Perhaps they have discovered her lies, and know I'll be back for her. Maybe the news story I saw was just a bait-and-hook to get me here. Maybe she did tell them the whole story, and that the fake one was part of the plan to make me confident enough to try and get her. Even if all that is true, I know she would willingly go with me – if I was able to get to her.

I'm on a street called Sycamore, trying to find a clue to where they are holding her. I had to take this man's house to stay off the street. I just needed a base for my research. This place made it, since there was only one old car that it had grass around it about a foot tall. All of the windows have dark- pull-down blinds, and there was a walker siting on the porch. All I did was quietly open the back door and walk right in. The guy was sleeping in a recliner. I merely picked up the heavy, glass ash tray that was sitting beside him and proceeded to crush his skull. I think he may have awakened for a second, but not long enough to know what was going on. As far as he knows, he died in his sleep. That's the dream isn't it? As far as I'm concerned, I did him a huge favor. I could tell by the general lack of housekeeping, that visitations were rare, if they existed at all.

Since then, I have been using his computer and television to find Heather. I have never witnessed such slow dial-up. This guy must have been a caveman or something. When trying to find a news story, I can almost go take a full piss before the page fully loads. As for the news stations on the TV, they have not been very helpful. The story is everywhere, but there are no real details. The only thing that sticks out to me as promising are a couple articles I found on the web. It looks like Heather will be a *Ward of the State* because of the experiences she has had. Her sister is living with her grandparents, but they don't seem interested in taking on that much responsibility. Hold on, Diary, I've just had an idea. I have been driving myself crazy trying to figure out a way to get her, but in writing to you, it is now clear.

No one knows my name. As far as anyone knows, I'm just another ordinary person. Maybe I could legitimately adopt her!! I mean, why not? I bet no one else will step up and do it. But, I bet that process takes forever, and especially for Heather, they are not likely to just put her in the adoption circuit. I need an *actual* plan. I like this idea, but how will it come together? This has to be how it is done. There's no way I can barge into a facility full of people and just take her, like I'm some kind of combat ninja. No, there has to be a smarter way. You know what? I don't even feel like killing anymore. Just thinking about this is giving me butterflies. I can see it now; me and her, father and daughter, fishing, cooking out, and…Hmm, even if they do decide to let her be adopted, there's no way a single man in his twenties would be able to adopt a female child. Damn…I guess I'll have to think of something else.

June 24, 2014 (1:25 p.m.)   Bowling Green, KY

NA

Dear Diary, I had a weird dream last night. I was sitting in a cave talking to some paintings. I don't think they were actually talking back, though. I talked to them and they just made strange noises. When they did, captions showed up under them as if they were on TV. I remember some of the text, which makes it even more intriguing. I vividly remember seeing the words *Frankfort Baby* written in green. It kept circling my mind this morning while I showered and ate breakfast. Yes, at the same time. Why not? After everything I've been through, why not eat an apple in the shower? But anyway, it wasn't until about noon that I realized how those two words related to my personal experience. I had to read back through some of my Diary, but there was a girl in Frankfort that I had a one night stand with – after killing her boyfriend. She had a baby. That's it, right there. I cannot adopt alone. If I had a wife with a baby, my chances for success would dramatically increase. It is only a couple hours away from here, so perhaps I'll go give it a shot. Wow, that would be great!

June 25, 2014 (11:00 a.m.)   Frankfort, KY

NA

Dear Diary, I arrived at her front doorstep last night. I had found a big jar of change in the old man's bedroom, so I used some of it to call a taxi from a pay phone, and the rest of it to pay for my trip here. I didn't realize how much change could fit into a half-gallon. I've decided to just walk away from murder all together. Why should I hide my face any longer? No one knows it was me, so I can just wash my hands of it and be an ordinary person. No one has any reason to suspect me for anything. At the beginning of my journey, I was a hollow shell of a person. I had no purpose and no emotions. This trip has been the therapy I needed. I have experienced love, anger, fear, and many other feelings. I now have a strong purpose in life. I need to form a family and get my daughter back. I still feel I'm a little unstable, but it's nothing I can't control.

Erica doesn't know my full intentions yet, because I don't want to spook her. She's the only person besides Heather who knows who I am. As far as she knows, I'm back in town and just *had* to see her again. When she opened the door, she immediately jumped up and gave me a big hug. It is like I was a long-lost love or something. She brought me in to say hi to little Evan. He was almost two, which is older than I had imagined. After that, we made love on the couch. It was indescribably intense. She was the instigator. I don't know where her passion comes from, but it must have something to do with me being the ultimate "bad boy." I'm under the impression that she had experienced so much abuse in her last relationship that my actions to save her had made me appear a superhero. I think she feels safe around me, because she believes I would kill someone if they ever tried to hurt her again. And, well, I guess I would. She is a very important piece of the puzzle.

June 26, 2014 (2:20 p.m.)   Frankfort, KY

NA

Dear Diary, I spent the night with her last night. I acted like my plans were to spend the day and go, but when she appeared sad, I asked her if she would like for me to spend the night. As we laid there in her bed, tangled up in each other, I began to realize this has been my destiny all along. Our bare bodies seemed to adhere together in the summer heat with only a window unit air-conditioner keeping us from overheating. I was awake long after she fell asleep. Erica's face was dimly lit by the green display on her bedside alarm clock. I watched her sleep and wondered if I could pull this off without accidentally hurting her. What if the cat came back? Can I resist harming Erica if he says he is hungry? I will have to. I have no choice. But anyway, back to her beauty. I have slept around before this night, with many others. However, it has always just been a task to appear as if I was "normal." I was never really interested in sex or the companionship of a significant other. I put my head back down in an attempt to doze off but her hair smelled of strawberries, and I just wanted to enjoy the moment. It's like I have just lost my virginity. It is hard to imagine I've lived my life this long without realizing the joy of emotions and feelings. It's just wonderful.

After we woke, I told her that I'm putting my past behind me, and all I want to do is live a normal, happy life with someone who wants a family. She looked at me with her welcoming eyes and said, "Well, I'm available." I leaned over to kiss her and it was official. We are a couple. I'm still holding off on the adoption thing until I know Heather is actually up for adoption. I don't really want Erica to know the whole story, that's why I keep this Diary so well hidden and only write on it when I'm alone. When the time is right, I'll let her know. Well, she's done getting Evan ready for the park, so I'm signing off.

June 26, 2014 (9:35 p.m.)   Frankfort, KY

NA

Dear Diary, I changed my first shitty diaper today. I didn't know what I was volunteering for. I thought it would be a good way to get some brownie points since I'm obviously going to end up moving in here with her. Erica was taking a bath and the kid blew ass during my shift. I asked him if he'd lost any vital organs and he just sat there mumbling something while pulling at his diaper. I poked my head into the bathroom to ask Erica where the diapers were. She looked very surprised at my willingness to step up as the dad. She told me where they were, and then it began. First off, Evan didn't want to be changed. He was just pulling at his diaper. There's no way sitting in that was comfortable. I had to let him play with the DVD remote while I changed him. I have smelled some pretty foul things over the last couple months, but his had to be one of the worst. It's almost like he shit, ate the shit, re-digested it, and then shit it again. I'm just glad my daughter was fully potty trained before she came into my life.

June 27, 2014 (8:40 p.m.)   Frankfort, KY

NA

Dear Diary, you are becoming a higher risk for me to keep. I was reading through some passages earlier and it hit me that everything I have ever done is contained in these pages. I want to burn you. I know burning you would be the best move. This is the only evidence there is. I have even gone into the back yard to do just that but I can't. I have tried, but for some reason I'm not allowed to do it. Why? Why can't I burn you? You are my worst enemy, because you are the only one who could ever tell on me. At any rate, there's no way I can continue to take these kinds of risks. The only way I can live the life I want, is to forget the life I had. I am better off as a person now. I know that my actions have sent me on the path that got me to this point. But I just cannot do it anymore. I have decided to bury you by a tree. Don't worry, I plan seal you water tight in plastic and bury you in a tin box. I do not want to see you anymore, but I don't want you to be destroyed either. So, I guess, if anyone is reading this…If the crimes within these pages are still unsolved, please destroy this Diary for me. I was not strong enough to do it myself. Goodbye my first true friend…

September 20, 2014 (1:35 a.m.)   Frankfort KY

Dear Diary, I can't do it anymore. I had to dig you up. I have to continue my journey. It has been about three months since we last spoke and I have missed you every day. My life with my instant family has been pretty good – for the most part. However, my feelings toward Erica have slowly begun to diminish. I don't know why, but it seems that the longer I am with her, the more bored I get of her. She is a great person, but I am not. I thought I could just live my life like a happy little fucking butterfly, but what the hell am I thinking? I don't deserve to be happy. Heather is in a children's home now, but there is no sign of adoption coming near. I'm almost afraid that if I wait too long, she will not remember me. Even if she does remember me, they may have her turned against me, and she wouldn't come with me.

I have brought the idea up to Erica, but she says she's content with what she has. I don't want to tell her that Heather is my daughter already. I just told her that I feel bad for orphans, and want to do a good deed. That doesn't matter anyway, because I got restless yesterday and called the children's home from a pay phone. I told them my wife and I were considering adoption, and that the girl from the TV seems like she might really need a good place to call home. The operator assured me that the girl is not likely to ever qualify for adoption, due to her mental status. She did tell me that her family has been visiting her more often, so if she is ever allowed to go with anyone, it would be with them. Diary, I just found this shit out, and I can't express my feelings in words. It has to be her grandparents. Perhaps they are starting to consider taking on the challenge. I have no choice but to go get Heather, but I have no idea *how*.

I had a dream about myself, Erica, Heather, and Evan. All of us were sitting happily around a fire, near a lake. I remember waking up, thinking that I couldn't wait for that to happen. Now I have to make a choice, though. It looks like it is either my daughter or the other two. Just writing it like that makes me realize my choice. I can't have it all, because Heather and I will not be able to live out in the open. If I am able to get her back, it is pretty much guaranteed that some blood will have been spilled in the process. I know she is good at laying low, but I'm not sure about Erica, and I know I can't bring a toddler along. I recognize that I cannot exist as a normal person and have what I want. I knew this day would come again. I knew I would have to get back to my roots. I can't even take a shower without closing my eyes and wishing it was blood running down my body, rather than water. I know the perfect temperature for the water to make it feel so very close to the sensation of blood. I miss the smell of it. I miss the shimmer of people's eyes as they die. I miss it all. I am starting to shake a little while writing this. It is not a nervous shake. It's more like being exhilarated. Just sitting here remembering it all is giving me goose bumps.

Perhaps the time I have spent with Erica has helped me clear my head and see the light. I read back over some of my Diary, and it seems that I was beginning to lose my mind. It is like I was completely losing touch with reality. The reality is that I love death and that death loves me. I cannot escape it and I need my travel buddy again. I hope she can still shoot.

September 21, 2014 (1:50 p.m.)
Bowling Green, KY

NA

Dear Diary, I did not waste any time getting here once my mind was made up. I did run into one slight problem though. Erica was not as open to letting me go as I thought she might. We stayed up most of the night talking, and I ended up just telling her that I cared for her and her son too much to put them at risk any longer. I told her that I got wind that the police might know who I am now, and are trying to look for me. I told her that if she was approached by anyone, to just deny everything. I asked her to destroy any pictures that I am in with her. She was willing to let me go, as long as I promised to come back some day if everything cools down. I told her I would. It was all a trick, Diary. The police are no closer to me than they are to the sun. With the couple months of no murders, it seems that people are starting to believe Heather's story. Erica dropped me off at the edge of the city this morning, and I have been walking around all day. I do not see the same police and military activity I saw last time I was in town.

I have even walked by the children's home where they are imprisoning Heather. I can feel the tension rising in my chest every time I look at that building. There are no bars or fences. There are no armed guards. This place is just a normal facility that isn't used to what I have to offer. I still don't know what to do, though. I can't just walk in there. I have found a patch of woods to sit in and think. I can see the building. I can also see a park. I think I'll just stay here for a while and see what unfolds.

September 21, 2014 (8:00 p.m.)
Bowling Green, KY

NA

Dear Diary, I have noticed the order in which cars have gone and come. I think I might know of one that belongs to some kind of social worker. Four times, she has gone to her car with a clipboard, left, and came back about an hour later. I have also noticed kids being brought out to the playground, yet not once did I see Heather. I think I'm going to have to find a way to use the social worker to get to her. I'm not sure how, but I'll sleep on it. She left for the last time around 6 p.m. and hasn't been back. I'm assuming she has clocked out and gone home. If her car is back tomorrow, then my theory will be correct and I she will be my ticket. Goodnight, Diary.

September 23, 2014 (11:40 p.m.)   Falco, AL

Woman, Husband, Girl (71)

Dear Diary, oh, what a trip! She is back in my arms once more. I can breathe again. She can't stop crying with joy, and I can't stop smiling. I bet you're curious to how. Well, when the social worker woman came back to work, I knew it would only be a matter of time before she left again. I waited until no one was in around, and I casually walked past her car to see if I could break in. She had a family car. When I lifted up on the handle, it was already unlocked. This was great. I quickly popped the trunk and jumped in. I made sure the release cord inside the trunk worked before I shut it completely behind me.

Sure enough, we were moving within the hour. I anticipated jumping out and threatening her to go get Heather and bring her to me, but that seemed crazy. Maybe crazy at first, but the more I thought about it, the more of an actual plan it became. But I couldn't very well just pop out *anywhere*, though. And how would I be sure that she wouldn't just call the police once she walked into the building. I had to wait in the trunk until after the end of her shift. Once six hit, we were moving again. After we parked, I waited for about an hour or so, just to make sure she was actually home, and not at a store or on a case. I pulled the cord and peaked out the trunk. I was in a garage. Talk about convenient. The door from the garage to the house was unlocked. I guess they thought that it was unnecessary, as long as the garage door was locked. I'm glad, too because I don't know how I would have gotten in if had been locked. I couldn't just knock on it! Having someone knock on that door from the garage would definitely alarm them.

Once through the door, I was in a hallway. I didn't know where I was going to get a weapon, or who was at the house. It's not really like me, but I was out of options. So, I decided to walk down the hall, opposite to where people were talking, in search of a weapon. I ended up in the kitchen, so the weapon of choice was obvious…They had a fucking full-sized, double-bladed axe just leaning up against the kitchen counter. It didn't make sense to me, until I saw the price tag hanging from the handle. It was new, and the Dad must have been on his way to take it out back, but had never made it past the refrigerator. At that point, I assumed that the dude must be a fat-ass, like I used to be. The convenience of this was an absolute sign that I was doing what I was supposed to. With the axe in hand, I tiptoed toward the voices. Sitting there on the couch, facing the television, was the woman, her husband, and a girl of about twenty. She must have been the daughter, still living at home or something. The living room was pretty spacious, and the couch was not up against a wall. Instead, the back was facing me, once I stepped into the room from the hall. When I was within swinging distance, I split the dad's head pretty much in half with one downward chop that was driven by all of my weight.

The two females started screaming and ran toward the TV. I freed the axe head, and demanded them to shut up and sit on the ground. I asked the crying social worker lady if she loved the girl she was holding onto. She cried, "Yes!" and I said, "Good, now listen to my directions." I explained to her that I would spend the night. Then, in the morning, she would go to work as normal, and work out a way to bring Heather here to me. She tried to deny that she had that ability, until I pulled her daughter across the floor and raised my axe. I told the lady that she could tell everyone that she'd gotten an urgent call from her grandparents about her sister being in the hospital, and that they are requesting to have her there. The woman actually seemed surprised that I knew so much about her. I told her that she will do this at all costs, even if she had to kidnap Heather when no one was looking. I told her that if I didn't see Heather within two hours after she goes to work, that her daughter's head would be looking just like her husband's when she returned that evening.

She agreed, and from there we just sat up all night and waited for morning. They tried asking me questions and begging me to just leave them alone. I didn't talk back to them. When they started to speak too loudly, or move too far away from the wall, I just tapped the axe on the floor, and they straightened right up. When the time came, I chopped off her husband's wedding ring finger, and told her to keep it in her front pocket, so she could feel it as she walked as a reminder to stick to the plan. She cried as I slid it in her pocket, and I told her

I'd check when she got home to make sure it was still there. It wasn't even an hour later that she walked through the door with Heather.

The depressed and dazed look on my daughter's face instantly disappeared when she saw me standing next to the dad's body. She ran to me as fast as her legs could carry her, and leapt into my arms. I held her and promised her I'd never let her go again. I apologized for trusting Abram, and I asked for her forgiveness. She began crying and put her wet face on my shoulder, squeezing me as hard as she could. The social worker was so stunned by Heather's instant return to sanity that she wasn't even thinking about her husband. She looked like a deer caught in the headlights. I asked Heather if she wanted to come with me. She nodded her head rapidly, and asked if she could have the girl by the wall. I guess it had been a while for her, too, so I let her have her fun. She asked where the kitchen was, and I pointed to the hall. The social worker woman was still stunned and didn't realize what was going on. The girl heard everything. She asked me what Heather was doing and what she was talking about.

All those questions were answered when she saw a little girl in a hospital gown running across the living room, wielding a steak knife. She was very fast. I'd almost forgotten how fast she was. The first cut went right into the daughter's neck, just above the shoulder. From there, it was just a barrage of stabbing. That scene snapped the mom out of her trance. She acted like she was planning to stop what was going on. When she tried to lunge at Heather, her face was welcomed with a Babe Ruth-quality axe strike to the nose. From there, Heather and I just gathered food and money from around the house, and then took off in the dad's truck. I just headed south and didn't stop, except once for gas. We drove for several hours, trying to get as far from that house as possible and we ended up here. Currently we are parked in a corn field. This seems to be bringing back memories for Heather. I wanted to ask her how she'd got the best of Abram, but I stayed away from the subject because I didn't want to hear any stories where she may have been abused. I just want to strike that from my mind, so I can maintain what little sanity I have left. Besides, I'm pretty sure my daughter wishes to forget it all, as well.

During our trip, I told her what my plans were for adoption, and why they'd never worked out. I told her how I have been a wreck ever since I lost her. She said that she would like to meet Erica one day, because she sounds really nice. It is weird seeing Heather again, especially as a girl. I almost feel like I'm seeing a ghost. Nonetheless, as she sits in the passenger seat scraping dry blood from her fingernails, I feel as if it is Christmas morning. God brought my daughter back to me. He brought her back from the dead and put her in my life once more. But, the feelings of starting a normal family in which I give up killing are long gone. I know that it is my destiny to continue. *Our* destiny to continue. If it was not chosen for us to do this, then why would I get Heather back? *Why?* While talking and writing, she has just told me she liked being Zach, and wants to go back being him. I agreed, because everyone will be looking for her even harder now. Next time we go to a house, I'll shorten and darken her hair again. I will never let anything happen to Heather again. I'll never trust another person besides her and Erica. Never!

September 24, 2014 (1:30 p.m.)   Falco, AL

Man, Woman, Old Man (74)

Dear Diary, I believe we have found the perfect place to lay low for a while. There are woods everywhere here. It seems like endless forests. There's no way they could find us here. Perhaps we could just live here forever. If it was just a little warmer out, we could just build a camp somewhere and never be found. But we just about froze while sleeping in the truck last night. I can't imagine spending another night out. I didn't think it ever got cold in the south, but I guess I was wrong. Well, I guess it isn't super-cold. Perhaps if I wasn't so concerned with Zach's wellbeing, I wouldn't have thought about it as much. Be that as it may, we decided to check into a farmhouse today. We passed a driveway after several miles of woods, and decided that it was secluded enough for our needs.

It was weird doing this again with Zach. The craziest part is that it was a farmhouse I lost her in, and now we're going back to one. However, I have learned much since then. I do not take chances anymore. People are inherently evil. I wouldn't call it a farmhouse. It is more of a double-wide, manufactured home sitting on a farm. We pulled in, and there were two children, both about 5, playing on a swing set. We saw no one else was outside until we pulled up near the front porch, where their van was. Then, this really fat woman wearing sweat pants and a hoodie walked out. She asked if we were lost. I got out and started talking to her, explaining how we were trying to find the nearest gas station, and that we had to pull in somewhere before we ran out and become stranded.

She began telling me directions – until Zach got out. The woman's gaze set upon him, and a look of fear swept over her. She looked like a deer caught in headlights. Then she whispered to herself, "Heather." Her cigarette fell from her open mouth. She looked back at me, started walking backward slowly, then turned and ran, yelling, "Jim!" I instinctively ran at her and tackled her to the ground. It was like wrestling a big, sweaty bear. Just as I got my hands around her neck and she was starting to black out, I took a boot to the face. It knocked me back on my ass. And then, a big hairy lumberjack-looking fucker jumped on my chest and started trying to punch me. All I could do was to hold my arms over my face. Then, all of a sudden, he stopped. I felt the familiar sensation of blood dripping onto my arms, so I slowly opened my guard and my eyes. The guy was too busy trying to stop all of his blood from leaving his neck to continue beating on me.

I didn't see anything hanging from his neck to provide evidence of how this had happened, but it was definitely gushing out quickly. It wasn't long before he fell over sideways and I was free. I was still a bit stunned by his kick, so it took me a minute to see what Zach was doing. Everything was still a bit blurry, but I could hear kids screaming for their mom. It was probably one of the most chilling sounds I have heard up to this point. I didn't really want to know what was going on, but my vision came back. I saw Zach standing beside the woman, who had been sliced from sternum to crotch. Most of her entrails were lying beside her. The boys were screaming because they were being forced at knife point to dig out the guts. They were both scooping from their mom as a dog digs in the sand. They were almost entirely drenched in blood, and Zach was standing there laughing.

I needed to go inside to make sure no one else was home. As I walked past the kids, I told Zach to make sure he doesn't hurt them. I reminded him that we don't hurt kids. He nodded his head and turned back to demand they dig faster. I walked into the house and went room to room. There was an elderly man, seemingly asleep in a hospital bed in a back room. He looked like he was nearing the end of his days and only buying minutes. I decided to help him along. I wanted it to be something quick and painless, as I sort of felt sorry for him lying there all by himself. Everyone he ever hung out with or looked up to is probably dead. It must suck to get that old and outlive everyone around you. Watching people die as plants do in the fall. I couldn't think of anything better than the axe, so I went back to the truck to retrieve it. Zach was still playing with the kids. I'm glad she is having fun. She deserves it, after everything she has been through. When I arrived beside the old man once more, I just chopped him in the forehead as hard as I could. He didn't even move. He never even knew he died. I mean, he obviously knew he was dying because he was old as shit, but there's no way he saw it coming when and how it did.

September 24, 2014 (8:25 p.m.)   Falco, AL

NA

Dear Diary, I called through the front door for Zach, after I knew the house was clear. I found a woman's wig in the master bedroom, and some makeup. I told Zach to not be alarmed once they were done playing, as I'd decided to come in for the evening to disguise myself. I showed him the wig, and he agreed. Honestly, I gave him a heads-up because I didn't want to get stabbed. I know he doesn't think before he acts. I put on the wig and a bunch of makeup. I thought I could do it fine, but I ended up just looking like a cross-dressed biker. I didn't realize how big my beard was becoming. How do you not notice something like that? What is wrong with me? I'll probably shave it after the kids go to bed.

They came in around dinnertime, and both of the boys were still crying. I get that they are sad about their parents, but at least they'd made a friend. I don't think they have ever seen another human being this far out in the wilderness. They didn't react to my disguise, but Zach dropped to the floor laughing. As long as I am able to keep my identity hidden from the kids, there should be no reason to hurt them. During the trip here, that was one of our big subjects for discussion. I told him that I would never let another living adult sleep in the same house as us, and he agreed to see the reason in my hard-wired decision not to hurt children. I explained that making good choices is one thing that separates us from wild animals. I think I'm going to have to get a mask for when kids are involved. From what I can tell, I am yet to be identified, so I'm not taking any chances. That makes me wonder what my family thinks about me never calling them. I wonder if they think I'm a missing victim. Maybe one day I'll go back for a visit.

Anyway, I found some peanut butter and jelly for dinner. Oh yeah, and I think I was able to cheer up the boys a little. Instead of having them take baths, I just had them stand in front of the kitchen sink while I sprayed them down with the sprayer thing. There was once a time that I cared a great deal about keeping a tidy house, but things have changed a bit. It did form a pretty large puddle of bloody water in the kitchen, so we had to eat in the living room. After we ate, I scavenged the house and found a shotgun. I can see how it would be handy, but it is too big for my needs. I decided to just stick with the axe for now. We are all watching cartoons now. Everyone has settled down, and I think I'll be getting them to bed soon.

September 24, 2014 (11:20 p.m.)   Falco, AL

NA

Dear Diary, the boys are asleep, but Zach is still up with me. I was able to find some beard trimmers, and shave his head. It was his idea to just go for a buzz cut. He said that there was a boy in the children's home with that style, and he thought it looked comfortable. He cuddled with me on the couch as we watched more TV. I think this is the most TV I have watched in a long time. This is also the most comfortable I have been in a long time. It is kind of hard to write like this, but I'm not giving up this quality time for anything. He is like a baby kitten right now. It's almost easy to forget what he is capable of. We really need to get him some new clothes. Now that I think of it, when's the last time I changed *my* clothes? Wow, this lifestyle choice is really stressful and time-consuming. I can hardly remember to follow through with the smallest hygienic routines.

I just remembered that there are bodies outside. Hmm, I hope they don't expect visitors tomorrow, because I'm not even trying to clean that up. Zach is mumbling now, he's finally asleep. I guess this is where we're sleeping tonight. I'm not complaining though. After losing your kid, the warmth of their cuddle is the most satisfying feeling imaginable. I just feel that I could live in this moment forever. I feel so bad for what he has been through. I can't even imagine what it was like to be held hostage by that sadistic freak, but nothing like that will ever happen again to him; not as long as I am alive and kicking. I'm getting off here now, it has been a long day and I still have a headache from the lumber jack. I'm sure glad Zach was quick to react, or dude would have ended up beating me to death. Goodnight.

September 25, 2014 (9:00 a.m.)　　　　　　　Falco, AL

NA

Dear Diary, I have been thinking. Why is it so hard for the police to catch me? They don't even know who I am yet. I am up to over 70 kills and I am far from an expert. Granted, I am getting better as I go, but it's not like I have any specialized training. So why am I free? I always thought it would be so hard to get away with murder. I thought that there was a scientific team of experts out there to track down murderers. I guess I am proving a point to myself – and everyone else – that murder is easy. It's almost like the only real way to get caught is to have a witness, leave obvious evidence, brag to someone, or turn yourself in. If you don't do any of those things, then you're free to kill whoever, whenever. I have come to my own conclusion that there is a reason why there are so many crime investigation shows on TV. It is because we need to be conditioned as a population that murder is hard. We need to be scared to commit murder because if everyone knew how easy it was, we would all be doing it.

Think about it… Everyone gets pissed at someone at some point. We think that we can't do anything about it because we'll end up in prison… Wrong… That's what they want us to think. The truth is, if you had a gun that you didn't mind smashing and trashing, you could just catch them walking to their car, shoot them, and move on with your life. No witnesses, no evidence, not a murderer. Perhaps there's a motive, but that doesn't mean shit. Everyone has a motive to kill someone. The truth is, as long as you don't tell your friends, and don't open your mouth in an investigation, there's nothing to go on. It is *that* easy. If you want to control a population that is stronger than the power that commands it, you need to condition them to believe you have unlimited power. So there. I'm living proof that this is true. I know my finger prints are fucked, giving me a natural advantage, but if not, all I'd need is gloves.

You know what's weird? When you dream, there's a world you live in until you wake. The dream world doesn't impact your reality, so if you can control your dream lucidly, you can do what you want and just wake up if things get too crazy. Then it is over. No matter how long or short your dream is, once it is over, it is over. I'm starting to think the same is true with our existence as humans. Our reality is what we make of it. We have rules and structure, but once we die, it is over. What is the difference between a person who did what they wanted, and a person who followed all the rules? Nothing; they're both dead. I'm pretty sure I've killed a few of each type by now. What if dying means that this is over, and nothing else? I'm treating this world as my dream world, and just waiting to wake up to whatever is next – even if it is nothing. Either way, I'm going to die eventually. In the world I have created for myself, I have removed all rules and social constraints. I have formed my own reality, and I have decided to live separate from the sheep. Zach is the only other person who can understand me. No one else would get it.

Anyway, I'm done rambling. I just haven't been this coherent in a long time. I figure I should get my thoughts on paper before something happens and I lose my mind again. Hopefully, reading this will help me snap out of it. The boys woke up crying a couple times last night, but it wasn't anything I couldn't sleep through. Like I said, I was exhausted. We all woke up this morning and now the boys are crying for their grandma. I guess they do see other people. I asked them if grandma comes over and they said yes. So it looks like we have a couple options. If we want to stay here for a while, we need to clean the mess out front and kill anyone who comes to the door. If we want to find somewhere else to go, we should leave soon. I'll talk it over with Zach after the laundry is done.

September 25, 2014 (4:20 p.m.)   Falco, AL

NA

Dear Diary, we did have a plan but it changed pretty fast. Zach and I went to the front yard to clean the mess the kids made. There was so much that we didn't even want to try. The woman looked like a gutted dear with about a 10-foot radius of body shrapnel surrounding her. The man has bled out completely and it drained down the inclined driveway for several feet. I figured Zach had something to do with the man's spontaneous neck leak. He verified this belief by telling me he had to stab the guy in the neck because he thought he was going to kill me. Actually, he's probably correct. I need to start thinking things through again. I understand that I have been through a lot lately and my mind has played tricks on me. But now I'm feeling relaxed and whole again. I need to start thinking before I act. When it was just me, I didn't really care to get caught or killed. Without my child, I had no reason to live. So what if I made a mistake and got caught.

Now though, I have someone to take care of and someone to be here for. I saw what became of him when I wasn't in the picture. He was rotting in a forgotten kids facility and his mind was starting to slip. Some of his stories about that place saddened me. I cannot continue to take chances. I cannot allow him to go back there. So, back to our revised plan. We are leaving. My mission of traveling from state to state however, is losing its luster. I don't think I'm the same person I used to be. I don't feel like the same person. I was an empty shell of a man with no emotion or links to reality. I had no reason to live and no passion for anything. Killing made me feel normal. The blood of my victims brought me peace. I get why I started my mission but why should I continue? Now I have a purpose, I can register emotion, I love another person unconditionally, and I don't really get the spiraling uncomfortable feeling in my body anymore. It seems that going through the tremendous loss of losing my child made me hit rock bottom. It was a pain worse than anything I have ever felt and there was nothing that was satisfying me. I was killing just to be killing and it felt good sometimes but all in all, I wasn't completely satisfied. Not like I am right now anyway.

What happened to me? Am I defined? I don't even know. All I know is I felt nothing, then I found peace in killing, then I found love in Zach, then I felt less than nothing after losing him. Now I'm fine so why kill anymore? This house has made me do a lot of thinking and I'm realizing that I cannot guarantee his safety with this lifestyle. I'm far from a professional, which is weird because my body count is higher than most professionals and my identity is still unknown. With that much practice; I'm still not an expert. So with that in mind, how is anyone an expert? Perhaps there are no killing experts. Perhaps it is just assumed that the ones who get away with it are pros because they haven't been caught. I'm probably considered a professional to the general public but that is far from true. I still think it is the law saying, "If we can't find him, then he must be a trained assassin." Well, dick, that's not at all correct. Perhaps you're just a fucking hack.

September 26, 2014 (5:10 p.m.)   Jackson, MS

NA

Dear Diary, we got cleaned up and left this morning. I stopped by a store on the way here and ran in to get some clothes and a few toys while he stayed in the vehicle. He still had the hospital gown because he was too big for the boy's clothes from the previous house. Speaking of the boys, I just took out all of the food from the cabinets and laid it on the floor for them. Zach locked them in the bedroom while I cleaned up and reverted back to my actual identity. He let them out and came to the van once I was in the driver's seat. I don't know how long it will take before they are looking for this van but I won't keep it long. Anyway, when I came out of the store with toys, Zach's face lit up like it was Easter morning. He changed in the back seat while I continued west. It made me feel good to see him back there playing with the action figures I got for him.

We've just been driving around trying to find a place to stay for a while. There is no doubt that they have figured out by now that Abram isn't me. They're probably upping their forces even more than ever. I don't even watch tv anymore because it is just the same shit over and over. Right now we're parked in front of a house for sale on Cox Street. It looks like a pretty good neighborhood. We decided to take a walk around the block earlier and it was surprisingly deserted. I bet everyone is afraid to come out because of me. Considering that, we hurried back to the van so we wouldn't stand out. I'm not sure what to do from here. Zach seems to be off in his own little world playing with his toys. He definitely doesn't talk as much as he used to. I know who he is but I'm starting to pick up on some subtle differences in his current vs. past personalities. There doesn't seem to be much of a soul left. His face is smiling and his voice is chipper but it is just now striking me that he hasn't stopped smiling ever since we reconnected. I originally thought that he was just very excited to see me but now it is starting to get a little creepy. Nothing can change how I feel about him but I think he needs a vacation from all of this before he loses his damn mind all together. But how do I give him a vacation when the only places we can sleep have dead people? We can't just rent a house and I'm not bringing this lifestyle to Erica and Evan. I don't know Diary. I'd rather see him eerily happy than locked up and depressed again. I guess I'm just stupid. I can't seem to do anything right. What the hell Diary? What the fuck?!

September 26, 2014 (11:40 p.m.) Jackson, MS

Woman (75)

Dear Diary, what the fuck ever! I'm done letting the world tell me what happy is and how to achieve it. I give up on thinking that I have to have a family, house, car, dog, and money to be fucking happy. I'm fucking happy! Don't I seem fucking happy? We were driving around and passed a park that had the perfect little family in it. The mom and dad were taking turns pushing their daughter on the swing with smiles from ear to ear. I could tell they didn't have a worry in the world. I wanted them dead. I wanted to take their place. The two thoughts crossed my mind at the same time and the thought of killing them brought me more joy than the thought of taking their place. It isn't envy, it is *hatred*. I hate everyone and no matter how hard I try to forget how cruel the world has been to me, I still hate it. That's not what I'm tripped out about though.

I asked Zach, who was just sitting in the passenger seat smiling out the window for no apparent reason, if he had any ideas on what we could do. He said he wanted to watch cartoons. I didn't know what else to do. I had to find a house to stay in. So I did what works, and pulled into a driveway on Florence Ave. He grabbed his knife and set up on his knees to look around for witnesses. He was much more eager than I was. It was clear so we just walked right up to the front door. I was going to convince them to open the door so I could use their phone since my van ran out of gas in their driveway. But Zach held up his arms and wanted me to hold him. I'm like, "Dude you're too big to be getting held." He said he had an idea. I went with it and held him. He laid his head on my shoulders and told me to tell them I found him lost and I needed the phone to call the police.

Well I did, and it worked. There was an older gentleman that answered the door and when he heard my story let me right in. His wife hopped up off the sofa and ran to us to ask if she could help in any way. He got down and held his hands up for her to hold him with a big sad face that no one could resist. This isn't where it got fucked up but it was a little surprising. We were all in the living room and the man handed me the phone. I heard a gasping sound and the woman's face looked as if she saw a ghost. The man asked, "Honey, is everything ok?" Suddenly, blood started running out her mouth and down Zach's shoulder. He never lifted his head. He looked like he was asleep. The man panicked because he didn't know what happened. I did though. I reached down and picked up a heavy ceramic dog from the end table. At the same time, the woman fell to her knees and then backward. The man was in a general panic but when Zach stood up and turned around, the guy screamed like a woman. It almost made me laugh but I held my composure. Zach had ruined a pair of his new clothes as he stood there with his stomach and lap covered in blood, holding his knife and smiling at the man. I then hit the old fucktard in the back of the head with the dog. It knocked him unconscious but didn't kill him, which surprised me due to the amount of blood he lost. I'm glad he didn't die because we need to know all we can about who comes here and what to expect. We may need him for answering phones or something.

Ok, now to the part that worries me a little. We tied up the husband and sat him beside the tv so we could watch him and cartoons at the same time. When he woke up, he just sat there sobbing. I asked him why he was so afraid of death. He said he wasn't afraid of death but his wife didn't deserve to go like that. He said she was such a wonderful and caring woman. I didn't listen to that bullshit for very long until I kicked him in the teeth and told him to stop fucking lying. I told him that no one is wonderful and the entire world is dark. I told him that I have witnessed the uncensored life of man and that people aren't themselves until they believe they are alone. I told him that I know he is full of shit and that he is evil too. I explained that I was a tool of God that is being used to extinguish evil. I mean, how else could I be so invincible and impervious to being caught? While

I was having this conversation, he begin to yell, "Stop!" I hit him in the head again to knock him out. When I turned around, I didn't know what to think. Zach was sitting there beside the wife, eating what appeared to be a raw piece of meat. Before I could ask where he got it, I noticed there was a strip of flesh about the size of a hot dog missing from the woman's outer thigh. I about puked. I told him to stop eating that. He lost his smile for the first time.

He dropped the meat and ran off to another room. I went after him because I felt bad that I reacted like that. He was in the office area, sitting by the wall crying. I went up to him and put my arm him to show him that I wasn't mad. I told him that I didn't mean to yell. I just didn't want him to eat people because it might make him sick. He turned around and cried on me. He pretty much just broke down and wouldn't stop crying. I didn't know what to say so I just held him until it passed. After about an hour, he wasn't moving so I looked down and he had fallen asleep. I carried him to the bedroom and put him to sleep on the bed and came back down here to catch up on my Diary. I don't understand why he was eating that woman. I'm assuming it has something to do with Abram. I also don't understand why he broke down like that but I feel it has something to do with everything he has been through. I am mad at myself for letting him be taken from me in the first place. If I would have just killed Abram, everything would be fine. I'm not sure what to do next. Fuck! The van. I need to go get it in the garage.

September 27, 2014 (3:55 a.m.)   Jackson, MS

NA

Dear Diary, I cannot sleep. The thought of Zach going through some kind of mental anguish is killing me. He also went to bed without eating. He has to be hungry. I feel so damn bad. I got used to not eating and running around not caring for myself. But he needs to have a normal diet. I don't even remember feeding him lately. He isn't just going to make his own food. What the hell is my problem? I can't rest with this on my mind. I have to wake him up and get him something to eat.

September 27, 2014 (1:20 p.m.)   Jackson, MS

NA

Dear Diary, I woke him up last night by bringing him breakfast in bed. I had eggs, toast, banana slices, and OJ. When he woke up, he had the smile back and ate everything I gave to him. He didn't say anything. I just sat at the edge of the bed and watched him eat. He crawled over and cuddled up beside me. I'm not going to bring up the meat eater thing again. I'm just going to forget it and hope that it was just a fluke. I will never let him go hungry again. I have to get my head on straight and re-learn what it is to be a dad. I have a second chance that people rarely receive and I need to do it right. In an attempt to bring him back to reality, I laid beside him and told him every bedtime story I knew. Interestingly, I got through them all in less than a half hour. He was fast asleep and I wasn't too far behind him. Upon waking, we went into the living room and the man was gone. In a panic, we both searched the house. We wanted to stay for a while but that would be impossible with a witness on the loose. We couldn't find him anywhere but Zach found the back door open and pieces of rope beside a kitchen knife. So it seems we have a witness. I'm writing this in an attempt to not freak out. I know where my mind goes when it is stressed, so I need to remain calm. I am controlling my breathing and getting ready to get the hell out of here.

September 27, 2014 (10:40 p.m.) Longview, TX

NA

Dear Diary, I am screwed. We are screwed. We got back into the van and just started driving west. We are now in Texas and there are police everywhere. We are sitting behind an abandoned house right now. If it works once, it could work again. I need to make it to a tv to see if they have identified me yet. I have never been concerned with the investigation until now. I need to know but how am I going to lay low and still watch tv? I thought about going into a restaurant or store but my face is probably everywhere by now. And what's worse, the witness will attest to Zach being a murderer. He will definitely get locked up if captured. He doesn't seem to be phased though. He is just sitting there playing with his action figures. I'm not sure what to do.

I told Zach that I don't know what to do and that I'm sorry for getting him into this. He told me that there's nothing to worry about and that we are warriors of the lord and he wouldn't let anything happen to us. I guess he's right but I still can't take chances. What if he's done with me? What if he is upset with me for letting Zach go hungry back there? The one advantage I have had is being unidentified. I wanted to slow down or stop killing because Zach needs to get away from it and I don't really need it anymore. But now what? What the hell is wrong with me? The instant I start getting my life together and start feeling like I might be able to stop doing this, I have to get identified. I just need to open my eyes and wake up. I guess our lives are getting ready to take a big turn. We will now need to kill everyone who sees our faces and that seems impossible. It is no longer about satisfaction. It is only about survival and maintaining our freedom. How can we change our identity?

What the fuck…? The cat is sitting on Zach's lap and he's petting it. Is he petting it or am I just seeing it? I don't know. How could he be petting it? I'll ask… Yeah, he confirms he sees it. Now I'm confused. Is the cat real? Is it an angel? Does he really see it or is he going with it because of his imagination? I cannot stop shaking as I watch the cat lick Zach's shirt while being groomed. I didn't ask the cat what he wanted because I was afraid he'd try to get me to hurt Zach and I would refuse. I'm not sure what happens if I refuse. I'm just staring and writing. Ok, I'm going to see what's up.

September 27, 2014 (11:30 p.m.) Longview, TX

NA

Dear Diary, we had a talk. I'm just going with it. Life is short enough already. Why would I want to live it in fear, confusion or pain? I don't know if the cat is real or if Zach sees him but the fact that it feels like he sees him makes me feel a little more connected. I told the cat, "I'm not hurting him." The cat told me he had no intentions on causing more pain to Zach. He told me that it was always his plan to reunite us. He said that he didn't show up on accident, that in every instance, he was pushing me along to get where I am. We talked for a bit and he vanished again, vowing to not come back now that I'm where I need to be. I don't know though. I have never trusted a cat. They have always made me a little uneasy. The only thing I'm sure about at this moment is that I need to keep Zach safe. I feel like my mind is going to explode right now. Zach seems like he's falling asleep so maybe I should do the same. I know I should do the same but I can't. How can I sleep now that everyone is going to know who we are? Why didn't I just kill the old man? I thought I learned my lesson about this. We cannot live where others are alive, especially now that we are going to be identified. Wait, it's Zach, not Heather. There's still a chance for Heather but Zach has killed in front of a living witness.

Maybe we should just change our identities. I could hold a makeup artist hostage until he makes us a disguise. No, that's idiotic. There's only one real solution here. We just need to kill everyone. Without people, we would be free forever. But, I cannot kill everyone. There are too many people. Zach's asleep now I think. I hope he is okay. I just want things back the way they used to be. He has changed a little. He just seems hollow. I used to be able to look into his eyes and feel him looking back at me but now, he seems lost. Don't get me wrong, he interacts with me just fine, it's just, I don't know, maybe I'm thinking about it too hard. He's probably fine. What I was saying is that we have no choice. We need to just stay on the road and stay in the dark. I miss taking him to Chuck-E-Cheese, stores, and museums. I miss being able to just walk into a hotel. Those days are gone as of right now. After I'm identified, everyone will memorize my face. Oh my God!! Fuck it all! I can't do this! I'm about to erupt and the only thing holding me still is watching him sleep. Why did I leave a fucking witness? I am so damn retarded. Whatever, I'm going to sleep. Fuck it. If I wake up free, we will continue our path. If I wake up to a cops face, I'll probably just kill myself. But wait. I can't kill myself. The only shred of sanity Zach possesses is due to being reunited with me. I remember his eyes when I got him back. They were dead. Not just hollow like now, but dead. I cannot do that to him again. If we are going to be caught, I have no other choice but to kill him first, then myself. Then we would meet again on the other side. We'll probably receive some kind of heaven award for being so committed to our mission. Oh well, that's fine. It sounds kind of nice actually. Good night.

September 28, 2014 (10:10 a.m.) Longview, TX

NA

Dear Diary, I am at a level of calm that I have never experienced. Last night, I gave up on everything. Without being identified, there was always a seeded fear about getting caught. I experienced an interesting epiphany that lifted the weight from my chest and the shackles from my legs. Zach has become my reflection. His emptiness is from my experience. I felt hollow my whole life. The only things that filled the void were murder and him. It seems that the only things that bring him joy are murder and me. He is not a mere shell, but in fact, my son. He looks to me for guidance and I have been torn on how to provide it. There was always a chance that I could find a way for us to settle down and become what I believed at the time, to be "normal." It was like I was two people in one body, constantly fighting and ridiculing each other for their differences. Not anymore. As I fell asleep I realized that there is no reason for that other person. That dream of living like everyone else died when I allowed a witness to live.

No, the only one here now is me. I have no struggle. I have no fight. Life was over before it started. I figured this out. It doesn't matter how long you live. It could be 8 years or 88 years but when you die, you're dead. In the whole scheme of things, both 8 and 88 are insignificant. There are only two main differences. The older one had more memories and had the chance to leave behind offspring. But how important is that? If one day, the world will become eaten by the sun, nothing we do now or in the future will mean anything. I woke up this morning from a very strange dream. I could actually control what I was doing. I knew I was dreaming while I was dreaming. My first reaction was to panic and try to wake myself up but after that didn't work, I tried to fly. It took a couple jumps but I was able to do it for a minute or so. I decided to run out into a street and shoot at random cars. I magically had a gun and began doing it, and then I woke. What I realized when I woke up was that nothing in my dream made a difference to this reality. Even though it felt real, once I woke, it wasn't. I could have lived by the rules or I could have done whatever I wanted and it wouldn't have mattered. I see this world as the dream and dying is the awakening. Sure I could play it safe but it wouldn't matter. I have settled on two things that allow us to be free. One is that none of this matters and the other is that we don't need to worry about getting caught because I'll kill us both and this dream would end.

September 28, 2014 (9:45 p.m.)   Pauls Valley, OK

Family (78)

Dear Diary, we drove around today looking for something to do. It didn't matter. We were just ready for something to keep us entertained. Oh, I should explain a little. No, we're not in the van. I'm sure they are looking for it by now. We just walked in the grass behind a row of houses until we found one that had the back door open. We walked right in and there was a teen age girl sitting at a computer straight across the dining room. I could tell Zach was eager to get started. I walked up quickly and planted the axe into the top of her head. There was a voice screaming on the computer. I realized pretty quickly why her attention wouldn't leave the screen. She was talking to someone online. It was a young boy and he was screaming franticly as he watched the blood run down her half split face. I could see a little screen on the corner that showed what he was seeing. It was centered mainly on her face. There was only a little bit of background. He could see my arm and that was about all. I turned the camera around so he couldn't see us and unplugged the computer.

After I freed the axe blade, we walked around the house looking for others. We could hear the shower going so we knew where someone was. We walked past the bathroom, peaking in all of the bedrooms. There was a man in his 30's still asleep. I hit him in the face with the blade and I don't think he experienced the slightest bit of pain. We then went back to the bathroom once we were certain the house was clear. Zach was getting very restless as he gripped his knife tightly. I told him he could have the next one. Luckily the bathroom door was unlocked. We entered quietly. The toilet was next to the tub sharing a wall with the showerhead. I flushed the toilet and she poked her head out to see who did it. Well, it wasn't who she expected. I grabbed her hair and pulled her face toward the toilet. Her body was fighting to keep its balance while it kicked at the slippery tub floor. Zach didn't do what he normally does with the quick slashes. Instead, he put the knifepoint on her jaw right between her upper and lower molars. As I continued to restrain her face to the toilet seat, he pushed the knife in slowly and through the other side, connecting with the toilet seat. He then started pulling toward her lips until the knife was free once more. He cut a groove in the seat during the process.

When that was over, he just stared at her smiling. I asked him if he was going to finish her because she was making too much noise. He ran the blade into each eye, not yet killing her. At this point, I realized he was just trying to have fun and be creative so I decided I would wait patiently until he was done. After everything he has been through, he needed a good release anyway. He dug around in their bathroom cabinet until he found a bottle of rubbing alcohol. He dumped it all over her face. I can't describe the sounds she was making but I'm sure you can imagine. He must have been bored with her though because his next move was his patented rapid stab to the body. I remembered that the kid on the computer must have called the cops by now, so we ran to the living room to find the keys to their family car hanging conveniently by the front door. That is how we got a car. After that, we just got onto 35 North until we ended up here. We're parked near a river by a green truck. I took this road because it looked like the only one without traffic. We're in the middle of a patch of woods. Zach has whispered to his knife once or twice during the trip. I think he might need to get some sleep or something. Why would anyone be here right now? It seems a little chilly to be fishing. I just remembered we haven't eaten yet. I'm getting off here to go find some food.

September 28, 2014 (11:40 p.m.) Pauls Valley, OK

Fisher (79)

Dear Diary, I think I'm a hunter now but I don't think I am legally able to tag my game. It stared by me thinking that the truck would have some food. The only things inside were cigarette butts and fast food wrappers. I thought that maybe, whoever owned the truck might still be around. I started using my hunter / gatherer instincts to hunt him down. At the edge of the pull off was nothing but a wall of thick weeds and woods. I saw where the weeds were disrupted in a line. We followed the path carefully until we came to the edge. Beyond that, we could see that there was a man with his pole in the September water. I knew that if we made any noises, he could spook and we'd miss our chance. I'm getting a little bored of the axe but it is definitely effective. While we sat in the edge of the weeds, we were still too far away to run at him with an axe. He would have plenty of time to run away.

I decided to make the human mating call to attract him into the trap. I disguised my voice as a female and made two really quick and mildly loud sex moans. I could seem through a space in the thicket but he could not see us. The man yelled out loud to demonstrate his dominance. He then made his way to us. When he was about five feet away from seeing us, I jumped out with the axe held high and full intention of landing a strike in the head. Instead, I slipped on some mud and fell forward. During my fall, the axe blade made contact with his boot, cutting his foot nearly in half. He wailed loudly in an attempt to get someone's attention. I jumped back to my feet and tackled him to the ground. I shoved my thumbs into his eye sockets and started slamming the back of his head on a nearby rock. I don't know how long it took him to die but when I finally stopped, I was pretty winded.

I looked up and Zach was already at the guys fishing spot digging through his supplies. He was very disappointed to find no food. Things are harder now that we can't just go to a store or drive through without the fear of being spotted. This must be what the pioneers felt like. We added wood to the pre-lit fire and talked for a little while. He told me about how he was kept as a slave in a basement of Abram's friend. The only time anyone went in there was to pleasure themselves. No one brought food or water. He was lucky enough that there was a leaky pipe that he could suck a bit of water through. He said there were a couple dead bodies just laying around. He found one that was fresh enough to still have meat on it. That is how he stayed alive.

I changed the subject before he got around to telling me how he got loose because it was only starting to bring up some anger and I have made up my mind that I am done with emotion. I wish to remain as I am now and continue moving forward. I didn't want Zach to feel like he was weird or to be ashamed of himself, so I offered to eat some of the fisherman with him. He went over and cut off a couple strips of meat while I prepared some roasting sticks. We roasted it over the fire until it was good and crispy. I have never considered doing this before but I was really hungry and there was no food in sight. I tried it and was amazed at how great it tasted. It was almost life changing. It had to be some of the best meat I have ever tried. When people die, they should be taken to a meat processing facility, not buried in the ground. I can now see how wasteful that is. While we sat there eating, he looked at me and began to laugh. I didn't know why he was laughing but it made me laugh too. I realized at that moment that my Zach was back. Something about him venting to me and turning me onto a new food brought him back. After we were done laughing, he walked over and lied beside me. He rested his head on my lap and looked up at me saying, "Promise you'll never let me go again." I promised him that as long as I'm kicking, no one that messes with him will be.

September 29, 2014 (8:05 p.m.)   Hot Springs, AR

Widow (80)

Dear Diary, I finally have a gun again. I don't even remember what happened to my last gun. I'm sure I could read back a couple pages but reflecting on the past won't bring it back. While flipping over the fisherman to get some of what Zach called, "The yummy back meat," I found a handgun. I don't know why he didn't have it drawn while he approached us. Lucky for me, and stupid of him. At any rate, here we sit in a graveyard. I feel we did a good deed today. Maybe Karma will give us some bonus points. We drove around for a minute trying to figure out what we were going to do next. I chose to pull into the graveyard because it seemed to be a place with the least amount of living people. We got out of the truck we confiscated from the river and started walking around. We needed the exercise. It is kind of fun reading all of the quotes and stories on the headstones.

About half way through the yard, there was a grieving old woman crying over a grave. We kept our distance because we were covered in too much mud and blood to be seen by anyone. We crouched down behind a large Jesus statue waiting for her to leave. She just kept crying and crying until she said, "Please God let me join my husband!" I knew then exactly why we had come here today. I looked at Zach, who was one step ahead of me and already had his knife drawn. I asked him for it because I wanted her to go quick and I'm not sure that's his style anymore. Once I had the knife, we walked up behind the woman saying, "Hello mam, God brought us here to answer your prayers." She was initially shocked to see us as we appeared, then confused at my statement, then scared when she saw the knife. I asked her why she was afraid, that this is what she asked for. She took a deep breath, then initiated a scream. Before she was at full volume, the handle was sticking out of her voice box.

She somehow had enough energy to run. As soon as she did, Zach ran after her and tackled her legs. He then climbed up her scrambling body and removed the cork. The knife must have been holding in all of the blood because there was hardly any until it was taken out. After that, it just flowed out like a fondue fountain. I dragged her by her feet back over to the site she was crying over so she could be with her husband. I laid her face down right on top of him. Now they were six feet apart and together forever. I'm not too concerned with someone finding her quickly because there are hardly any stones around with fresh flowers. Something tells me it isn't exactly the most frequented location in the town.

You know what Diary, we're hungry and though people are tasty, I'd like to keep that to a one time deal back there. I know there's a chance I'm identified but there's also a chance that I am not. Even if the guy had a good description, there's no way everyone knows about it. So perhaps I could take him out to a restaurant and have fun one more time before it is too late and I am a household face to everyone. Yeah, I think we deserve some fun.

September 29, 2014 (11:00 p.m.) Atlanta, GA

Boy (81)

Dear Diary, I am very excited today because I have figured out how to reward Zach for everything he has been through. I haven't told him yet because I want it to be a surprise but I'll tell you. I'm planning a trip to a theme park in Orlando. I thought of the idea while we were sitting there in the graveyard and a grey cat was playing with a ball cap that must have become lost in the wind. I snickered and thought of Cat in the Hat. At that moment I knew what I had to do. I don't know if they have they'll have Cat in the Hat there but for some reason it made me think of it. Before everyone knows who I am, and I'm hoping they don't already, we need a vacation. This job is harder than you might think. I jumped right up and said, "C'mon." He eagerly followed as we jumped into the only other car around. It must have belonged to the widow because the keys were still in it. I felt like we were driving in class during the whole trip here in a big black Lincoln.

During the drive, I started to realize that we needed to be clean and that we needed money. It's not like I can just go in and kill people for their tickets. We got as far as Atlanta before the gas light came on. When scoping for a house, we had a couple factors to look for. We needed to find one that looked like the owner had money and we needed two people about our size so we could get some clothes. I know I have always had a thing for not killing kids but I can't seem to understand the reasoning anymore. I know I should feel something against it but I just don't. It's like age, gender and species have all blended together for me. I could kill or eat any of them. In fact, the only person on this planet that means anything to me right now is my son. Everyone and everything else can just lay down and bleed to death. The more I think about it, people are just another kind of livestock. The only real difference is that I can understand what they are saying when they talk. If a chicken knew how to talk, people would probably stop killing and eating them.

But for me, it is actually not that complicated. The words that come out of someone's mouth are different than what they actually mean or think. Just in saying "Lost in Translation," I know that I don't understand the soul of a human any more than the soul of a frog. For this reason, kids just seem like veil to me now. But anyway, back to my original story. We found a good target on a road called Dragon Place. We drove past the house a couple times before committing to it. Conveniently, there was a man on the front porch about my size talking to a boy just a little bigger than Zach. We avoided driving back past too much because I didn't want anyone to get suspicious. We found a place to park about a block away and sat until we thought they may have gone back inside. We left the car there and walked toward the house, hoping no one would see us and rush out to check if we were injured or something.

Once we were close enough to see the porch, Zach held my hand tightly and started walking slower. I asked him why he was hesitating. He exclaimed that here was a kid in the target house and he didn't think we would be able to do this without hurting him. I told him I'm done worrying about that. He seemed confused but I asked him, "What's the difference between the chicken and the egg?" He said, "One has feathers." I said, "Nope, it's the taste." He chuckled a bit and asked if we were planning to hurt him too. I told him everyone dies someday and there's no better day than the one we're walking in. He loosened his grip and put some pep in his step.

When we came to the house, the sun was no longer visible. We sat on the front step to figure out how to get in but before we could consider our options, the answer was behind us. The dad opened the door and demanded to know why we were on his porch. He looked angry but there was no fear in his eyes. He noticed I was with a child, so there's no way we were a threat. I rose to my feet and pointed the gun in his face and said, "Just a glass of water and we'll be on our way." He changed his tone very quickly into a sobbing little girl. I'm starting to get annoyed with people's tears. They used to bring me joy but not anymore. Now they just get on my nerves. I feel embarrassed for them. It's like they really thought they were going to live for all eternity until the moment they're faced with death. Why is it such a surprise to everyone? How can they live their life knowing they will die but never really accepting it? It's just weird.

Anyway, we walked into the house after him and by then he had already figured out who we were. He asked me to spare his family and that if I needed to take a life tonight, he would go as long as I left his family alone. That was actually pretty brave for someone who started off the night with baby tears. But I simply told him that he would be dying regardless of his willingness to participate. The crying began again. Around the corner ran the boy, Zach lunged at him and sunk his knife into his chest. The boy looked very upset that this just happened to him, but it wasn't but a few seconds before he wasn't worried at all. The dad lost his damn mind so I pistol-whipped him upside the head with all my might. He dropped to the ground but still kept yelling "Jason! No! Why!" I'm like, "Why the fuck not? He might have grown up to be a rapist or something." I kicked him in the side of the head because apparently the whole gun thing doesn't work that well on some people. It still didn't knock him out.

I think the guy was getting his energy from an overload of adrenalin or something but he just flat out refused to get knocked out. In my amazement, I didn't realize that there was a woman in the living room balled up into a corner, shaking and begging me to stop. Must have been the wife. I became curious to how far she would go to save her husband. I asked Zach to bring me some veil. He laughed at our inside joke. The dad was still conscious at this point but just barely. I didn't feel concerned about walking away from him for a minute. Zach handed me a strip of flesh and I brought it to the woman. I told her that if she would eat some son, the father shall live. She refused as she freaked out some more. I made her sit up against the wall and I sat the meat in her lap. I slowly began to walk toward the man while she watched. I said, "On the count of three, he dies if you don't eat." I don't understand why it was such a difficult decision. I mean, it's not like eating it would have made any real difference. Right before I got to three, I had the gun inside of dudes mouth with the hammer pulled back. She screamed that she would do it just to let them live. So I sat on his back and watched her eat her whole serving. I said, "Now rank that from 1 to 10 where 1 is like eating cat shit and 10 being the best thing she's ever eaten."

She didn't know what to say and I could only guess her thought process. I could see that she would want to say 1 because she didn't enjoy eating her son that much at all. Then I could see her saying 10 because he was hers and 1 would have been an insult. She didn't want to give me a number so I started counting again. She told me 5. I guess that's fair, I mean it's not like it was cooked or anything. If I would have had time to cook it, I'm sure she would have given it a better review. Right now, I'm still sitting here on his back hitting him every once in a while when he moves too much. The woman has already puked four times and is laying down facing the corner of the wall. Zach is laying on the couch. I'm not sure if he is asleep or not but I haven't heard him say anything for about 20 minutes. I don't know what to do here. Don't get me wrong, they will die I just don't know how. The reason it is important to me is because I feel I have been very wasteful lately. I used to really enjoy killing people. It used to make me feel so good inside. But I'm just numb now. I can't really register if I feel good or bad. Before I started all of this, I felt really bad but at least it was something. I would do anything just to feel that. I can register emotions such as anger but I can't seem to really feel anything to the fullest. Maybe I'll have fun with these ones and try to bring that spark back into my life.

September 30, 2014 (1:40 p.m.)   Atlanta, GA

Mom/Dad (83)

Dear Diary, am I evil? I don't think I am but sometimes I feel like I am. I know I'm doing the right thing here. If you think about it, I'm actually helping the planet. So, I guess I'm probably an environmental activist in a way. People damage the planet, and I kill the people. Maybe Mother Nature is the one who called on me to rid her of some of the parasites that bore into her skin on a daily basis. Last night, the mom and dad died. First it was the dad since he was nearly there anyway. While the mom lay there shaking, now in a kitchen corner, I rolled the dad over and smacked him in the face a couple times until he woke up. I decided to watch the eyes to see if it brings me any sensations. He looked over to his son and tried to scream but I put the gun barrel in his throat until he was mute. He asked what I did to his wife. I told them that she was fine and that I believed she was asleep on the floor.

I then got a good idea for an experiment. I told him that his wife would live if he did exactly as I directed and he agreed. I helped him into a sitting position and asked where they kept the flour. He looked very confused but he told me that it was stored in the top left cabinet. I found a large unopened bag of All-Purpose flour. My goal was to test if it was actually for all purposes. Could one of the purposes be murder? Well, I sat it in front of him and walked over to the wife holding a knife I pulled from a drawer. Before I started, I decided that Zach would like to see it as well. I yelled into the living room for him and he rushed around the corner. I asked him if he thought this man would be able to eat that whole bag of flour without stopping for a drink. He laughed and said he didn't think it would be possible. The guy heard this and immediately chimed in that we were crazy and that there is no way of pulling that off.

I took a clock off of the wall and placed it on the floor between us. As I was explaining the rules, the woman rolled over to face us. They cried in each other's direction about how much they loved one another. It was almost enough to turn my stomach. I said that he had five minutes to finish the flour, or the wife would have her throat slit. I could tell that he considered arguing with me until he looked at his son, which reminded him of the weight of the situation. He started scooping it by the handful and shoving it into his mouth. He was doing really great at first but then his mouth and throat were dry. The flour started clogging in his throat is what I believe he was yelling at me. He was only about half way into the bag at that point. Every time he breathed, flour dust clouds escaped his nose and mouth. What's funny to me is that he believed I would spare them so much that he put himself through all of that. Toward the end of his life, he was completely stopped up with a solid cork of flour in his throat. His face was beginning to turn reddish-purple from the lack of oxygen but he kept shoving it in his mouth and shoving it down his throat with his finger.

I have never seen so much determination to save another. I think he honestly believed that as long as he could live enough to finish the bag, that I'd spare her. He sacrificed himself for her. I guess he did care. The whole time he was playing the game, Zach was sitting there wide eyed with his excited face on. Also, the mom kept pleading for her husband to stop. She pleaded with me to stop him. Suddenly, he paused and fell to his side. With flour everywhere and his cheeks stuffed with full, he reminded me of a chipmunk ghost. I wanted to be excited about seeing it. I know it was fun to watch but it wasn't like it should have been.

I then put my attention onto the woman. I dragged her by her feet into their basement, which was actually a wine cellar. That excited me a little. Zach shut the door, since he was the last one down. I asked Zach for his knife because I left mine up stairs. He handed it to me and I asked him if he still remembered how to play *tic-tac-toe*. Once he confirmed that he did, I tried to find something to tie the woman down with. This is the first place I've ever been to that doesn't have rope, tape, chains or wires. Absolutely nothing I could find to tie her down. I ended up using some kind of press thing to secure her hands. I don't know what it is but I'm sure it has something to do with making wine. Perhaps it's a grape press. It is like a wooden barrel with a flat piece that presses down into the barrel as you twist the handle on top. I knocked off a couple pieces of wood on the press so I could get her hands into it.

I had to hold her hands in while Zach twisted the handle. Since the barrel was on the floor, she had to go to her knees and put her hands out in a praying position. As the flat piece made contact with her hands, she started screaming full force. I don't know why people scream. What does it benefit? I could hear he bones staring to crunch all together and I told Zach it was secure. I gave it another quarter turn myself just to make sure it was good and snug. After that, I cut her shirt off and scribed a tic-tac-toe board on her left shoulder blade. While we took turns with the knife playing our game, it became hard to read what we were writing because of the blood covering our handwriting. I opened a bottle of wine and dumped some on her back to clear the blood. We played 3 games before we realized that he was just going to beat me every time we played. Of course I let him win, but I didn't let him know that. It was cute watching him get excited about winning something.

The woman was nearly silent by the end of the third game. I think she finally began to realize the pointlessness of a human scream. I wanted to see in her eyes and feel the blood at the same time just to see if I could feel something. No matter how I tried to arrange myself, I couldn't figure out how to see in her eyes and feel the blood at the same time so I decided to just go with feeling it this time. With her assistance, I was able to lift the barrel to a tabletop so she was able to stand. It was too heavy for her to move by herself so I wasn't concerned with an escape or any kind of self-defense. I got down to my underwear so I could feel it on my bare skin. I laid on my back and wiggled my way between her feet until her crotch was over my chest. I told Zach to start making cuts all around her so we could get the blood flowing. He did as I asked and I was taking a warm shower in blood. With each new slice, it was like the water pressure was being increased. I rolled over to my belly and let it run onto my back. It started to pool up around me as well. I crawled back and forth a couple times so I could give myself a good glaze.

She stood there screaming, but that didn't last long. She tried to drop to her knees but with her hands stuck, she never made it fully to the ground. I just relaxed there until the blood slowed to a drip. I did feel something. It took a lot of work, but I did have a sensation. It was like a warm, comfortable feeling rushed from my nuts to the top of my head. Just to see if I could take it a step further, I asked for the knife while I was lying on my back. It seemed like it would be funny to see from the outside looking in because I resembled a car mechanic asking for a tool to work on his car. I sliced under her belly button from one side to the other, forming a big abdominal smile. Her guts were free to spill out onto my chest and face. I remained there for a couple minutes but quickly realized that it did nothing for me. I guess intestines are not my thing. When I crawled out from under her, Zach said that he wanted to try it. I told him next time he can. But as for me, I needed a good shower. The feeling lasted for a minute or so but after that, I was just covered in a mess that needed cleaned up. I don't really know if it is even that important to have sensation anyway. It seems like a lot of work to go through for something so insignificant. I think I'm fine just hanging with my kid and staying busy on the road delivering the world from the pesky ass vermin.

September 30, 2014 (10:30 p.m.) Atlanta, GA

N/A

Dear Diary, I decided to just spend the night here and get an early start to the theme park tomorrow. The good news is that I don't have to worry about killing anyone for a ticket in the parking lot like I was considering. These people had plenty of money for us to be comfortable for a while. They were sneaky about it though. They had a floor safe but it didn't have anything in it but personal files and pictures. It seems like the perfect place for money if it needed to be stored. So, I was kind of aggravated at that. I then kicked their clothes hamper in frustration. When it fell over, some clothes fell out and so did a couple twenty-dollar bills. I dumped out the hamper and hit the jackpot. I found $3,112 hidden in the bottom of that thing. It is like they were prepared for a break in. If a burglar came in, they would probably just grab the safe. I mean, who hides money under their dirty clothes? It seemed kind of genius actually.

We decided to celebrate by ordering pizza. Not giving a shit seems to be good for my stress level. Since we're already known, I don't care if the delivery guy identifies us after the fact. I did have Zach answer the door though; just to be sure I wasn't recognized on the spot. We ordered two large pizzas and a couple subs. The plan is to have some leftovers. It was pretty amazing to enjoy this day with him. It reminded me of the good days, when we didn't have a worry in the world. We just watched TV while enjoying our pizza and wine. I'm pretty happy right now. This is what life is supposed to be like. It is us against the world and we're winning. Tomorrow will be awesome and he has no idea. I hope they sell funnel cakes there because that's my favorite.

October 1, 2014 (10:55 p.m.)   Orlando, FL

N/A

Dear Diary, we woke up around 5 a.m. and set off on the way here in the family SUV. We packed enough food and clothes to get us through anything that comes our way. When we started to see signs, Zach said he wished we could go there. I had to tell him at that point. When I did, he about flipped out. He was so excited that he was up on his knees counting mile markers. I told him that it was his birthday party since I wasn't able to be there for him when he turned nine. He completely forgot that he had a birthday some months back. That made him even more excited. When we arrived, we were able to buy tickets up front with cash. I had fun but this was mainly for him to get a break. We stayed the whole day and worked our way around the entire park. We ate there and I bought him whatever souvenir he wanted. We were elbow to elbow with other people and I didn't have to kill anyone. It was such a relief to wander unnoticed and without purpose. I don't think anyone would have recognized me even if there was a billboard with my face on it. They were too consumed with their own enjoyment to even take note of their surroundings.

I have to admit that every couple minutes; I was imagining good ways to take people out. For instance, in one of the attractions, there was quite a bit of darkness. I thought to myself, "If I had a knife on me, how many throats could I slice before people caught on?" In the end I didn't hurt anyone because I was there for my boy and I didn't want to do anything to cut the day short. Seeing him so happy for a whole day was so rewarding to me. I actually considered the thought of going back to Erica and doing the family thing again. That was just a short thought though because the reality is that there is no chance for that without extreme plastic surgery or disguises. That's not the life I want to live. I would rather be in control than spend every day of my life as someone I'm not.

Yeah, so the park was fun and we needed a place to stay that wouldn't identify us. I also didn't want to kill anyone on our day off so luckily I found a bed and breakfast. The owners are two old ladies that look like they stopped checking the news when colored pixels were introduced to the general public. All we had to do was walk in and hand them some money, and that was it. It was a bit weird, as if we had traveled back in time. As I sit here on this flower-patterned bed, I am tossing around the idea of just staying here for a while. Zach is in the bed beside mine passed out already. He had a very full day today. I'll sleep on it thought. Talk to you tomorrow.

October 2, 2014 (9:40 p.m.)   Orlando, FL

2 Women (85)

Dear Diary, I have decided to stay just for a couple days. There is a lake right out back and I think I have found secret bait that works great. I was going to talk it over with Zach this morning but when I woke, he was gone. I went into an instant panic as I fell into an Abram flashback. I busted through the bedroom door and ran down the steps yelling for him. It isn't like him to not be in sight when I wake up. He is usually up before me but he will stay laying down until I wake up. I rushed into the kitchen, hoping to see the women serving him breakfast but it was empty. My heart felt like it was about to pound out of my chest and I started to get a little dizzy. I yelled for him once more and he responded with, "In here!"

His voice was coming from down the hall. I didn't know why he would be in a different bedroom but I was just happy to know he was alive. When I opened the door, I realized he was in the hosts' room. He was lying between them in their bed. I think they were a couple to be sharing a bed. Anyway, he was on his back with his hands behind his head and his ankles crossed. He was absolutely covered in blood from head to toe. I could hardly recognize the women, which helped me realize how long he had been in there working on them. I knew I should have been shocked or something but I wasn't. I was just upset he left the room without telling me. I was also a little concerned with his actions. Why did he need to kill them? This was not my wish. I'm starting to think he is getting a little insubordinate but he's just a kid and I think they all go through these stages. He must be trying to express himself or find his own identity. I know how fragile he is emotionally so I did not talk to him about it. I decided to just wait it out and reinforce the importance of not leaving my side before we go to bed every night.

I was impressed with the amount of flesh he was able to remove from their bones. I asked him what he was doing with the meat. He told me it was in the refrigerator. On my way to the kitchen to check it out, I realized there was a blood and gristle trail from the bed to the fridge. I must have been too worried about Zach to see it before. But, he had thrown most of the food that was in the fridge onto the floor to make room. The fridge was pretty well packed with slabs and chunks of meat. He didn't even wrap it or put it in Tupperware. He just threw it on the racks. I knew a bit more about meat preservation than he did, so I called him into the kitchen to show him how to wash and store meat. I explained that you could keep out about a three-day supply in the fridge but the rest needed to be put in freezer bags and stored in the freezer. Luckily they had a large deep freezer.

There was a lot to go through so I gave him the job of washing and I bagged. I thought it was cute seeing him there glazed in red as he developed a new skill. When we were done, his hands were clean up to his elbows but rest of him was not. We both thought he looked funny so he went up to take a shower and change. I'm definitely glad we have so much extra clothing now. I know we should not keep the SUV but is so perfect for all of our traveling supplies. I'm not too concerned right now though because the driveway here is surrounded by trees, to create ambience. It is pretty well hidden at the moment. Ok, I almost forgot to explain my secret bait. We had a couple pounds of meat that wouldn't fit into the freezer. While bagging the meat, I saw the lake. I cut up all the extra into what appeared to be stew meat and took him fishing after he was all cleaned up. There were several poles in their shed. We caught a couple bass and several catfish. A couple days ago, I would have wanted to keep the fish but I'm slowly starting to be turned off on the thought of eating any other meat than human. He agreed and we just made the evening catch and release.

There was an old man down about twenty yards away who was not having the same luck as we were. He made a couple comedic comments about our bait but then walked over to ask what we were using as bait. Zach appeared to be nervous when the man asked but the resemblance to dear meat was uncanny. I told him it was venison stew meat. He offered to pay for some but I kindly gave him a handful at no cost. I wanted some karma points. He felt obligated to stay for a quick chat so I allowed it. He asked if we were staying at the bed and breakfast and I told him yes. He went on and on about how nice the women were there and how one was actually a childhood friend. There was about a fifty percent chance he was hooking a piece of her on his line as he rambled about his admiration for her. I enjoyed the irony in it. For dinner, we found some stuffing in the cabinet. We had old lady steaks and stuffing. I can't get over how great this meat is. It isn't like it just fills me up like a hamburger. It seems to have addictive qualities because I feel very comfortable after eating it. I am beginning to realize why it is illegal to eat. This must be the forbidden fruit the serpent gave to Eve. I bet there was just a dead body behind a bush and the snake said, "Hey, come take a bite of this."

October 3, 2014 (1:35 p.m.)   Orlando, FL

N/A

Dear Diary, last night was great. After dinner, we spent much of the night relaxing by the lake catching catfish. I was a little confused however, at Zach's routine of stabbing the fish in the head before throwing them back in. In fact, that is the main reason I decided it was time to go in. The floating fish corpses really started to add up quickly. We discussed staying for a while and we both agreed that it seemed like a perfect place to lay low. We spent most of this morning cleaning the path from the bedroom door to the kitchen. We tried but had to lay a path of rugs and towels to cover it. We decided we will allow guests into the bed and breakfast and run it as we own it. Of course we will be killing some of our customers but the higher risk people will be treated as royalty and released.

As of now, the closed sign is still on the door and we have not answered any phone calls. We are still trying to work out a couple kinks. One of which, is the fact that someone who comes in could recognize me since I'm sure my identity is known. Another, is coming up with a reason the women aren't working. Maybe someone will come in that knows them. Maybe they have friends. No matter, though. I'm not really that concerned at the moment.

October 3, 2014 (9:45 p.m.)   Orlando, FL

N/A

So we have our first customers. We could probably fit more but since we aren't that familiar with running a bed and breakfast, we wanted to start slow. It feels kinda right doing this. No more than ten minutes after we opened for business, 3 college age girls walked through the door giggling about some guy at the beach. That reminds me; we should go to the beach this summer. Zach and I were all cleaned up and looking like we belonged behind the front desk. The tallest one spoke to me first, saying they wanted to stay for two nights. I looked at the computer and pretended to type something. She gave me a credit card and I just slid it under the monitor. I didn't see a credit card slot anywhere so I just improvised. It's not like we're really in it for the money anyway.

I asked Zach to show them to their room and he did. The girls thought it was so cute that my son was working here with me. When he came back down, he asked when we get to kill them. I told him that we're going to try to avoid it. He didn't seem pleased but he nodded and went into the kitchen. I hurried over to put the closed sign back up. They stayed in their room for a couple hours and all I could hear was laughter. They must be drunk. Who the fuck laughs that much. I wanted to kill them for a second. Anyway, I started to hear a scratching sound from under the computer. I jumped because I didn't know what kind of creepy animals they have around here. I knocked over the monitor and held up my fists. There was nothing. As soon as I realized there was nothing, my heart started to pound and I had tunnel vision. I thought I was going to die.

I sat down in the chair and tried to calm myself back down. I could see something moving in the screen but it was unplugged when I knocked it over. I didn't have any choice but to look closer. Suddenly, my eyes focused and I saw the cats face staring back at me. I asked him how he got into the computer. His reply, "I'm a wizard, duh." I asked him why he was back and he told me to go into the kitchen. He then disappeared and my panic faded out. I got up and walked into the kitchen. Zach was sitting in the corner of the room with blood running from his knees. He had pulled up his pants and started cutting his knees with a kitchen knife. I sat down beside him and asked him why he was hurting himself. I held my hand out for the knife and he gave it to me. He looked at me with tears in his eyes and said, "You love them more than me."

I had a talk with him, explaining that he was my son and that no one could ever replace him. Trust me, I tried… I didn't tell him that part though. He still wasn't convinced. He's under the impression that I must care a lot for someone if I let them live. Do all parents have to go through this kind of emotional crap? All I know is that I don't want to lose him again and I recalled life without him. I told him that if he really feels that way, we can kill them tonight but he had to promise not to cut himself ever again. I took him upstairs to the room we're staying in and cleaned up his cuts. I don't think he needs any butterfly stitches or anything but I did have to wrap both of his knees. I don't know why he chose that as an option. The knees? I understand the arms and wrist. I guess kids will always keep you guessing.

October 4, 2014 (7:10 a.m.)   Orlando, FL

3 Girls (88)

Ok, we're done here. Zach is rounding up the food and then we're out. When we went to bed, Zach was pumped about what we were going to do. I wasn't as worked up as he was. I could care less anymore. I told him not to leave the room without me and to wake me at 3 a.m. I sorta wanted him to fall asleep waiting for the time but he didn't. Right at 3 a.m. he started shaking me to wake me up. He kept telling me it was time. I swear you would think Santa just came here or something. I grabbed my knife from the nightstand and asked him where his was. He lifted up his shirt to reveal its hiding place. He was eager to go. We walked slowly out our door, hoping not to wake anyone with the squeaky hinges. He was getting restless with how long it was taking me to open the door. I explained that if we wake them, then we can't do it. There are too many. He nodded in understating and waited patiently for me to create an exit wide enough to slip through.

From there, it was just one carefully planted step after another. The floors were all squeaky. What the hell? We found out that if you step beside something heavy, there is no sound. I guess it is because the heavy item is already pushing the floorboards down. We strategically made our way to their room, which was not locked. I repeated the same process for opening their door. They were all asleep. Two in one bed, and one in the other. The one who paid was the one seeping alone. I began wondering what their story was. Zach tried to make his way to the bed with two girls but I redirected him to go to the bed with one. He said it wasn't fair that I got more. I told him that it is because I'm bigger and if they put up a fight, I'll be better equipped to handle it. He accepted my answer and moved on.

I let him go first since he was so excited about it. He just started stabbing in the throat and face area as quickly as he could. I think the girl tried to wake for a split second but that ended quickly. One of my girls rolled over, I think because of the sound. I jammed the knife into the side of her head and she was gone. I did end up giving the last to Zach though. He did the same thing again with the rapid stabbing. I was going to ask him if he was happy but he got up on the bed with the one and lay down with her. I was still a little dazed from being awaken so I wanted to return the favor. I cut open the stomach of one of my girls and grabbed a hunk of something out of her. I had to cut so it would release. I tossed it and hit him in the side of the face. He rose quickly and I said, "Food fight!" He laughed loudly and sliced his open. He dug out the entrails and returned fire.

We got carried away in the fun. Everything in the room was covered. We also ran out into the other areas of the house looking for each other. It was almost like a messy tag. Someone would hide and the other would hit them with a piece of flesh when they discovered the hiding spot. When we were done, I was happy that he was so happy but there is absolutely no way of cleaning this mess. He's actually been ready for a couple minutes as I write this, so I'm getting off here and we'll talk again after we end up somewhere. Not sure where though. Side note; I asked him to get food and all he has is a big bag of old lady meat. I guess I have to go look for myself. We can't live on meat alone. We do still have food in the SUV I think. Ahh, no more rambling. We need to get out of here.

October 4, 2014 (7:15 p.m.)   White Oak, SC

Doesn't Matter

Dear Diary, I'm done counting kills. I don't care anymore. This is just my life. There is no reason. I know I have become popular lately but this is a little ridiculous. They pretty much have police check points everywhere. I don't know how they have funded such a search. Zach and I were traveling toward South Carolina to find a place to hang low for a while. After about an hour of driving, I had to stop for gas. I had him go in and pay because I didn't want anyone to notice me. When he came out, he was saying that he overheard some women talking about a killer being in the area and that they had a checkpoint up the road. I figured that the SUV had to have been identified as missing, so we had to ditch it. We drove a couple more miles up until we came to a rest area.

People are used to seeing cars parked at those places for long periods of time, so we left it there. We had sat there for no more than thirty minutes, when a semi pulled in. I wasn't going to target him because I know truckers can be difficult people to deal with but I saw that he got out with a boy about eleven years old. At that point, I knew I had a vice. When they went into the bathrooms, Zach and I grabbed everything we could from the SUV and threw it into the back of the trailer. They were hauling eggs. I've never seen so many eggs. When they came out, I was sitting on the curb near the truck and Zach was hiding on the other side. I called to the guy before he got in and asked him if he knew how far the next town was. When he was distracted by offering directions, Zach came in from the back and grabbed the boy's head while simultaneously pulling it back and putting the knife to his throat. I tried not to laugh as the boy stumbled backward. Zach was a bit smaller than him so when the boy's head was forced back to Zach's level, he was hardly able to sustain his balance.

The man held his hands up and told his son to play it cool. I explained to him that he was going to get us to South Carolina and everyone would be safe. He agreed with whatever I said but seemed uncomfortable when I told him I would be hiding in the back with the boy. He told the kid to just do whatever I said and it'll be ok. I handed Zach the gun since he would be up front. He needed more protection than me. I took the boy and we hid between some racks of eggs. Before the door was shut behind us, I told the man that if anyone besides him opened the trailer door, the boy would die.

During the trip, we were stopped for checks three different times. I could kind of hear what was going on. They said they were looking for a killer and to be careful. They didn't look in the trailer though. I think that the cops were looking for something other than a truck driver and a boy. We pulled up at the edge of a town. The trucker opened the back and told me we were in South Carolina. I peaked out but told him we need to be somewhere residential with no cities. He shut the door again and when he opened it once more, we were parked along a small street with nothing but trees. I was glad to finally stop because the boy did nothing but whimper the whole trip. I looked out and it seemed fine for the moment. There were very few cars going by. I told him to come in with us and I'll go. He jumped up into the trailer and made his way back to his son. I looked again for cars. There were none, so I pulled out my gun and shot them both in the facial area. If you've never shot a gun in the back of a trailer, don't do it. That shit is loud. I mean, think of a gunshot and then multiply that by fifty. It must have been because of how enclosed the area was.

I toppled a couple racks of eggs over onto them and jumped out, shutting the door behind me. In the cab, I found a pen with some paper. I wrote in all caps so caps, "Dead battery. Walked into town for another. Please don't tow." I placed this in the window seal and threw the keys into the woods. It seemed like a good plan because if a cop checked out the truck for being suspicious, he may give it a couple more hours before making anything out of it. If nothing else, he'd just write a ticket or something. I noticed a padlock in the glove box too so I put it on the trailer door to decrease the potential of the bodies being found before we had a place to stay.

We walked through the woods, packing all we could carry. We came to a road called Patrick. Zach was carrying the bag of meat and was complaining because it was starting to get warm. I had him drop it. I told him that it was the easiest food source in the world to find and that there's no reason to keep leftovers. He reluctantly tossed it into the ditch as we walked down the road. Luckily for us, an old man in a pickup truck stopped to see if we needed a ride. I think he figured I was a trustworthy person since I was walking with a kid, carrying bags of clothes. I don't remember what happened to my axe though. I didn't have it and neither did Zach. It's like I know I had it but don't remember the last place I had it. This is starting to get old. Anyway, the man looked friendly enough but so did Abram. I was by the window and Zach was in the middle. I kept my eye on the man hoping he wouldn't try anything funny.

He asked where we were going and I told him that we were just trying to find a place for the night because the tow truck took our car but wouldn't take us. He was appalled that a person would leave a man and child stranded like that. He said he had a guesthouse we were welcome to stay in until the car was fixed. This man's generosity reminded me of Abram so much. It must have reminded Zach of him too. We were traveling about forty MPH when Zach just started laughing. The man and I were both confused but the laugh was so contagious that we ended up joining in for no reason. Just as soon as the man had his mouth wide open to release a belly laugh, Zach jammed his knife straight into his mouth and through the back of his neck with tremendous accuracy. He is getting good. I was impressed with his precision but concerned that we were now swerving back and forth with an incapacitated driver. I had enough awareness to grab the wheel and keep us from hitting any trees. I pretty much kept it on the road but we weren't slowing down. Zach was just sitting up on his knees twisting the knife back and forth. I told him to hit the break but he didn't know which one.

He dropped to the floor and I told him it was the biggest one. He held the break down with his hand until we came to a complete stop. We sat there for a couple minutes as the man let out his last couple twitches. We're sitting at a pull off right now so I can calm my nerves by writing. I swear Diary, if I didn't have you, I'm sure I would be dead or insane by now. Well, I guess we should just keep driving. I mean, we have a truck now.

October 4, 2014 (11:50 p.m.)   Pineville, NC

Dear Diary, fucking checkpoints are pissing me off. We have decided to just go back to the original goal and hit all fifty states. The plan is to just drive through them and randomly shoot a person from the truck. We would just keep driving and sleep in the bed of the truck on top of our new clothes. However, we can't even go into another state without a fucking checkpoint. Am I seriously that damn popular? Why won't they just let it go already? I don't see why they are so insistent on bringing me in. People die every day. I'm not doing anything that freak'n wrong.

So, right before we got into North Carolina, we came to the tail end of a long traffic jam, which turned out to be a check point. As soon as I spotted a line of flashing red and blue lights in the distance, I pulled off to the side by the wood line. I knew that this would appear as suspicious to onlookers so I quickly grabbed a t-shirt from my bag and a lighter from the man's cup holder. I popped the hood and casually walked to the front and pushed the shirt down with the motor. I lit it on fire and once it was going good, I shook it down there a little to put out the flame but keep it smoldering and smoking. I walked to Zach's side of the truck. It now looked like our truck was broken down and possibly overheating. Right behind us was a tall thicket of plant life. From the angle of the road and where we were parked, we were able to get down and crawl into the woods through the thicket without being noticed. We had to leave everything we couldn't carry or stick in our pockets while crawling. Now all we have is money, two knives, a handgun, and a couple boxes of ammo.

We sprinted through the woods, following the road from a distance. We had to hurry because it would only be a few moments before someone thought to inspect the truck and find the guy laying across the seat. It was funny traveling while sitting on someone though. It was like a weird booster seat. As we passed the traffic stop, I could barely see through the woods but I didn't hear any dogs. Also, I didn't see any helicopters. This makes me believe that the check points are routine over here. If they really knew I was near, they would have called in the cavalry. We decided to stay off the roads for a while. We turned away from the road and ran further into the woods. We passed over a road but I couldn't see its name anywhere. We just kept walking. I figured that there's less chance of being caught if we're off the main drag. We came to a row of houses pretty spaciously parted but there was no way through without jumping a fence.

I looked for signs of vacancy with the absence of dogs when choosing a yard to cross. We found one that looked like the grass hasn't been cut for about a week and decided to cross over. When we got closer to the house, I peered around the corner to see if there were any cars in the driveway. There were none. We listened and looked through the back windows and it appeared that no one was home. We were pretty much out of sight of the neighbors and we were planning to just bust through the back door to stay to rest. However, we noticed there ware alarm stickers on the windows. I looked at the upstairs windows and there were no stickers. I remembered someone telling me at some point that upper windows are typically left without alarms. I told Zach to look for a ladder. I was obviously looking in the wrong spot because Zach motioned for me to come to the shed nestled in the back corner of the yard. There was a padlock on it but he said he believed there would be a ladder in there if anywhere.

I couldn't think of a good way to get into the shed without making too much noise. I eventually decided to just open the barn style door as much as I could, stick in a sturdy stick that I found in the yard, and pry it open until the locking mechanism ripped out. This wasn't as loud as I thought it would be so my anxiety simmered down quickly. He was right; there was a tall sliding ladder. I raised it up to the second floor windows and climbed up. I took another quick look around for witnesses before trying to get it open. There were none. I was able to push the middle part of the window in far enough to pop it out of the lock. Once I was in, I signaled for Zach to follow. It was very difficult, but we managed to get the ladder up through the window. I didn't want anyone noticing it outside, and I wanted to be sure we had a silent exit. I'm just glad they don't have motion detectors anywhere.

This will be our home until the family gets back. It has everything we need except for cold food. The cabinets are packed but they made sure to leave their fridge empty before leaving. The tv works and Zach has just been munching on junk food and watching cartoons all evening. I spent a while in the bathroom shaving and showering. I didn't realize how much better I look now. I'm actually getting into shape a little. Perhaps it is all of the body dragging I've been doing. They say you're supposed to do body weights to build muscle. Oh, I just realized something. It is nearly Halloween. I never really enjoyed it myself but I'm sure Zach will be ecstatic. What would he wear? I know? Perhaps we can cover ourselves in real blood and carry the knives around. Ha, yes... That will be hilarious. I'm out. I need to get some sleep. All of this walking has really gotten to my legs.

October 5, 2014 (2:00 p.m.)   Pineville, NC

Dear Diary, I told Zach about Halloween and my costume idea. Needless to say, he absolutely loves it. When we woke, I was tasked with finding something for breakfast. It ended up being dry cereal from the box and a cup of sink water. It wasn't that satisfying. All I can think about is getting my teeth into a big hunk of meat. The house has no sign of children but perhaps a teenager. There a 3 rooms, one is obviously the parent's and one almost looks like a college dorm with all of the class paraphernalia posted all over the walls. Definitely a boy because of the swimsuit model poster on the closet door. The remaining bedroom is just for storing random junk. No plans to do anything today Diary. We're both very exhausted. I think it's just eating and TV today.

October 7, 2014 (3:30 p.m.)   Pineville, NC

Dear Diary, sorry I didn't write yesterday but it was just a repeat of the day prior. There is nothing exciting here. There is nothing to make me feel good. Zach is in the same boat. He has been very moody and all he can talk about is getting some meat. I agree with him on this. I can't stop thinking about it either. It's like I didn't realize what I had until it was gone. It's like a drug that you don't realize you're hooked on. No wonder every animal in the world wants to eat us. We are addictive. At least I don't have it as bad as Zach though. I noticed him fiddling with his knife once and accidentally cut his finger. He stopped the blood by sucking on it. Until then, he was very on edge but once the blood was in his mouth, he relaxed almost immediately. I knew I had to do something quick or he may start doing that as a behavior.

Don't let Zach know because I told him he shouldn't do it. But, seeing him relaxed like that gave me the idea to try it. I went into the bathroom where he couldn't see and put a small cut on my palm. I then let it drip into my mouth and yes, I felt peaceful afterward. I can't do that anymore though because he might catch me doing it and I don't want to set a bad example for him. Well, just talking about this is giving me an appetite and I can't shake it. This feeling reminds me of how I used to feel before I started my journey.

October 7, 2014 (4:45 p.m.)   Pineville, NC

Dear Diary, I think they have finally discovered the truck I left. I heard a knock on the front door. Zach and I froze and remained silent until we believed they were gone. I squinted to see through a little string hole on the front blinds. I knew that moving the blinds would show that someone was home. I noticed several police cars parked along the street. I thought they knew where we were but I was comforted to see officers walking from door to door on both sides of the street. Why did I have to find harbor so close to the last crime scene? Why am I so fucking stupid? I'm glad we got the ladder up. That would have been the end right there. How are we supposed to leave now? We can't. We just have to stay here.

October 7, 2014 (8:50 p.m.)   Pineville, NC

Dear Diary, I think our prayers were answered a while ago. We were just sitting on the couch when we heard a couple car doors slam. I thought it was the police again and went to the string hole. It was the family returning from their trip. I scurried to the kitchen to retrieve my gun, and then went back to the front door. I hid so that the door swung open and I was behind it. Zach was following my orders to stay hidden in the bedroom. The dad walked in first and was pissed. He saw food and trash laying everywhere. His wife and teen followed him in quickly. It seems they were under the impression that their house was burglarized. The dad said, "That woman is going to get it!" I don't know why he assumed the vandal was a woman but whatever.

When they were completely in the house, I slammed the front door and aimed my gun at them. I demanded that they get to the ground or I would shoot them, starting with the teen. They did as I asked but begged and pleaded like everyone else. I have become numb to all of that shit though. I used to find joy in it but now it is just part of the job. They were all carrying several grocery bags each. We can survive off of them for a while. At least until the coast is clear and we're able to leave. The mom asked if I was the killer everyone was looking for. I was confused by her question because if she watches the news, she should know what I look like. However, I don't remember the last time I watched the news so I told her no. I said that I was trying to rob the house but they walked in and caught me. I told her that if they did what I said, no one would be hurt. I asked the mom what she did for a living. She said schoolteacher. I asked the same question to the dad and he said police officer.

I about shit my pants. He is a police officer and didn't know my identity. I handed them the phone one at a time and told them to call work and leave messages that there was a family emergency and they will not be returning for another week. They did as I asked. I then had the mom call the school and say the same thing for her son. Now we have the house and no one should be looking for them. I wonder if they know they're dying soon.

October 8, 2014 (7:30 p.m.)   Pineville, NC

Dear Diary, last night was pretty good. We had the Allen family play UNO with their teeth. At gun point, Zach had them sit on their wooden dining room chairs while I nailed their hands to the sides. 3 nails per hand for the adults and 2 nails for the teen. We placed bowls under their hands to catch the blood while we all sat around the dimly lit table. They kept crying and begging but it is just white noise. As long as they can bleed, I think I'll keep them alive. It was funny playing cards with them but it took forever for them to draw cards with their teeth. The smartest was the dad, who used his nose to pull cards from the deck. After our second game Zach checked the hands and confirmed that the draining had stopped. When we poured it all together, we each had a coffee cup full. I honestly thought there would be more than that.

This would be a first for both of us and I was a bit nervous. I wondered what it would taste like in bulk like this. It just made since that if small amounts of blood from our hand relieves tension, that this would be very nice. We said cheers and drank it all in front of the Allens. They appeared to be appalled but they can't be expected to understand. It was very calming. It was thick and warm. It almost felt like I was eating tomato soup. About an hour after our card game was over, the dad called Zach by the name Heather and Zach looked at him surprised. That is when our identities were no longer hidden from them. Until then, he was doing the least amount of sobbing. The moment Zach reacted to being called Heather; the dad began crying like a child. He knew that this would be the end of the Allens. He knew that there was no longer a potential for release. He told his wife and son that he loved them and that he will search for them in heaven.

While he did that, I began to realize that I was hungry and that Zach may be as well. I sliced one of the woman's calves off the bone. The dad tried to be a hero by pulling his hands away from the chair, leaving the nails behind. Luckily Zach had been standing behind him with the hammer and he wacked him on the back of the head before he stood up. That knocked him out but didn't kill him. I hurried to tightly wrap the mom's leg with towels so she wouldn't bleed to death. The son fainted as soon as I started to cut his mom's leg. I took a large mirror off the wall in the dining room and removed the hanging wire. I stretched it across the dad's neck tightly and nailed down the ends on both sides. I didn't want Mr. big man to do anything crazy again.

I sliced the meat into thin strips and fried it with some mushroom, onion, and brown gravy that were still in the grocery bags. I had completely forgotten about the bags in the living room. Everything seemed to be good except the dairy products. While we ate at the table, the son and dad had awakened but the mom was passed out. We offered the son a bowl and he turned it down. I guess he is too good for mom soup. I bet she would have been offended if she wasn't asleep.

After we were filled up, we put the left overs in the fridge. Everyone was awake and just sad looking. The dad tried to remove the wire from his neck a couple times but it was too tight. We left them in the dining room and went to the front room to watch some tv.

While Zach watched cartoons, I couldn't stop thinking about how Mr. Allen, a Police Officer, didn't know my identity. The witness had to have reported us by now. I couldn't let it go so I went back to talk with him for a while. They were still where I left them. I asked him what he knew about me. He said that my identity is still unknown and that every department everywhere is fully staffed in the search. He said that they know I travel but can't seem to figure out where I'll strike next. He said that the only witness was a kid, who provided a description that looks nothing like me. Apparently Zach is supposed to be an innocent slave of mine. What a laugh.

I pushed harder for answers. I asked him what he knew about my trip to Mississippi. He told me everything he could recall. It seems that the man I thought escaped, only made it to the neighbor's yard before dying from injuries. I can't explain the relief I experienced from that conversation. There was so much weight taken off my chest to know that Zach and I can once again walk among the living. I pretty much skipped into the next room. I prepared him for the good news by shutting off the tv and sitting in front of him. I explained what I had just found out but he didn't really have a reaction. He was just happy the old guy was dead. It's like he doesn't have one clue about what being caught would mean for us. I'm concerned that at this point, criminal scientists would probably want to dissect me for study.

We decided to take shifts watching the family. I let him sleep through the night and right before daylight, I woke him so I could get some shuteye. It was about 11a.m. before I woke to the sounds of screaming. I jumped up and ran into the kitchen, where Zach was laying under the mom's chair naked and completely covered in blood. It looked like she had just been born or something. I panicked because I thought he was injured. I ran to pull him out and when I did, he was laughing. His mouth and eyes were wide open. Blood had glazed his teeth and the white of his eyes. I gave him a little shake to snap him out of it. When he had relaxed, I held him tight and looked back at the chair. He had sliced the woman's stomach open from left spine all the way around to right spine. The boy and dad were erratic. I hadn't noticed them until then. I never asked Zach what happened because I remember doing it myself and he wanted a turn. I completely forgot about my promise so I guess he took it upon himself to do it. Oh well, there's still two left. I sat Zach in the tub and turned on the shower. He sat there with his knees folded up and his head resting on top of them.

I asked him how it felt for him and he said it was amazing. I'm glad he had fun but while he sat in the tub scrubbing off, I had to go clean his mess. Luckily, the Allens had a lot of freezer space. I had to use grocery store and trash bags to keep all of the meat in though. I haven't ever seen anyone who doesn't keep freezer bags in their house. To skin and clean her, I had to put her on the dining room table. It took about an hour or so to get all I could. I can't really describe the facial expressions and sounds coming from the son and husband. I guess to picture it; you'd have to put yourself in their shoes. That is something I have never really been able to do though. How do you feel what someone else is feeling? I have come close but mostly I just guess how they feel and that's as far as it goes.

I started to smell something stinky so I looked at the boy, who had apparently shit his pants a time or two. I forgot he was still nailed to the chair. I couldn't help but to laugh at him for it. I nicknamed him shit britches. I'm honestly at a loss on what to do with these two now. We have plenty of food to last us a couple days. Anyway, after Zach and I were all cleaned up, we returned to the tv. It was so hard to find a show without special bulletins about me. I didn't watch them though. I'm not really interested in all of that cop drama bullshit. I'm living my life out of the box and if I get involved in the news, I'm going to be easier to control. Nope, I could care less what they say about me as long as they don't know who I am. But what about the old man we fished with? Surely he could at least give our descriptions as probable. He must have not considered us as suspect or he is afraid to come forward since we know where he lives.

By the time lunch came around, I realized that we hadn't eaten any greens for a while so we just ate salad. Zach tried to refuse but I explained how it would make him grow up strong and how he would be able to choke someone with his bare hands. That inspired him enough for seconds. It's like the old Popeye cartoons telling kids that all they had to do is eat spinach and they could knock big guys out with a single punch. I noticed how hard the boy was staring at our plates as we ate so I made him a plate. He had to eat it like a dog but he finished it all. The dad then asked if he could be let up. He promised not to do anything stupid. He said he forgives us for killing his wife and that he just wants to be safe with his son. He said he would never tell anyone of our identity.

I'm not an idiot. I know he was trying his academy crap. Making promises and trying to help me recognize that him and his son are not too much different from me and my son. Maybe then, I'd acquire compassion and turn my back so he could eat me. Hell no, I wasn't born yesterday. Just for trying that shit, I found some pliers and removed his two upper and lower front teeth. So, four teeth altogether. I explained to him the whole time why he wouldn't be able to get into my head. Really, the only reason he's still alive is so we can have something to do later. We haven't figured it out yet but we will. Right now, we're just relaxing in the front room watching an old Batman show.

October 8, 2014 (11:10 p.m.)   Pineville, NC

Dear Diary, I think I'm a metal head now. We spent some time rummaging through the house looking for supplies when I came to the teen's stereo system. He had a Rob Zombie CD sitting out and I thought it looked interesting. I put it in and listened to the song Dragula or Dracula or something like that. Well, I started getting very excited. I turned it up as loud as it would go and I started to actually see different colors. It has to be the music. As the CD played, I had the urge to chop someone up. I asked Zach what he thought of it and he gave me two thumbs up as he was head banging. I went to the kitchen drawers and took every utensil into the dining room. I dumped them by the dad, or Levi as he called himself. It took two trips because they had a lot of utensils.

As I sat there and stared at his bewildered face, I started to get less excited. I went back to stereo, unplugged it and took it to the dining room. I then sat it on the table beside the pile of mother and turned it back on. When the music came back on, I started to get energized again. We made up a game kind of like Hot Potato or Jinga. Zach and I would grab a utensil of our choice and stab Levi wherever we wanted. The goal was to not be the person who last stabbed when he died. Get it? So strategically we cut off his clothes and started with the feet. I explained to the dad that his rules were simple. If he resisted in any way, we would stick that utensil into his son. He agreed to the rules and he laid still. Zach went first and tried to grab a spoon. I laughed as he tried to dig it into ankle. I guess he thought that the more dull an instrument, the less likely he would be of delivering the fatal blow.

He gave up and grabbed a fork, which he easily jammed into the bottom of the foot. I'm so ticklish that it made my nuts jerk when I saw it. The dad flinched but did not resist. He just kept staring at his son as they cried stories back and forth to each other. When I took my turn, I went straight for the steak knife and stuck it right beside the shinbone. My method relied on staying away from major arteries and keeping my cuts as clean as possible. Zach's strategy was to stay on the extremities, using all of the forks. By the time we got to the knees and elbows, he had already passed out twice and his son had 3 forks in his leg. I don't know how much silverware was hanging out of the dad but we didn't move inward until we were out of room.

He had pretty much given up on life and pain by the time the CD was over, but he was still not dead. We ran out of utensils before we made it to his shoulders. Well, everything except the spoons. We didn't want to give up, so we walked around finding anything a little sharp.

We formed a pile of pens, pencils, and picture frames we broke into shanks. Without going into too much detail, Zach ended up winning. I had a piece of wood that was much bigger than I wanted. To make matters worse, the only places I had to choose from were the face, neck, chest, and stomach. I attempted to run it into the esophagus bit it splintered in half and got his jugular vein. As he bled out and convulsed, I tried to rush Zach to take his turn. He kept peaking back at the body as he pretended to search for his utensil. He did that until the shaking stopped and jumped up in victory. That was an extremely long game but it kept us entertained.

October 9, 2014 (3:30 p.m.)   Pineville, NC

Dear Diary, the fucking basement. Why didn't I check the basement? If I would have, I wouldn't have been so startled when she just walked into the door. Early this morning, some live-in aunt walked in while Zach and I were sleeping. I took the recliner so he could have the couch. Well, she walked in with a night bag and didn't notice we were there until she had shut and locked the door. We woke quickly and she stood there in shock. She was short with black stringy hair, holding an unlit cigarette between her lips. She said loudly, "Now who the hell are you?" "Levi, you didn't tell me we had guests!" She didn't see the mess in the dining room so I told her we were friends just staying in for a couple days. She didn't look pleased but turned the opposite of the dining room and opened what I though was a closet door. She walked in and down to her basement room mumbling about her brother being an idiot.

Zach and I looked at each other confused and tried to figure out what just happened. We were still dazed and it was hard to process information. We just sat there wondering if she was going to come back up. Suddenly I realized that the boy was still at the table. We didn't want him to make any sounds to alarm her so we ran in to check him out. He was in pretty bad shape, resting his head on the table, whispering something faint. He looked extremely dehydrated and sad. I decided to put him out of his misery by simply slicing his throat. He had suffered enough. It was time to move on to something else.

We stood by the door holding the knives we pulled from daddy pin cushion and listened as she grumbled down stairs about losing her money at bingo. Better yet, how bingo robbed her. I opened the door and yelled down asking if she wanted breakfast. She said yes and I went into the kitchen to cook a family meal… From the family… Ha. Zach stood watch at the corner while I warmed up some of the left over mom and gravy. We both walked down with the meal and sat it on her dresser while she was digging in her bag trying to find something. We watched her eat it all before we told her what it was. She was talking about it as if it was the greatest thing she has ever eaten and wanted the recipe.

I told her to follow me up stairs and I'd show her my secret ingredient. When we came close to the corner, I stepped aside and let her walk in front. When she walked in in saw the grizzly scene, she shuttered loudly. Her fight or flight kicked in and she ran after me swinging rapidly in a windmill fashion. I stepped to the right and tripped her as she passed me. I then pulled her hair back as my knee compressed her spine. I was going to kill her but remembered that I had never taught my boy to throw a punch. I asked him if he wanted to learn and he nodded eagerly. I held her hands out one at a time and stuck a hole in each palm. While I did this, I asked Zach to remove the shoe strings from the boy's shoes. He did as I asked. I ran the string through her hands and sat her back facing the heavy table leg that I then tied her hands to. She was yelling every cuss word she had learned since first grade. I could swear she called me a momma's boy at some point.

I showed Zach how to swing a punch the first time and I about broke the nose. He followed my lead. For a kid, he has a pretty good punch. I told him to aim for the nose and the chin. He had to do it from a crouched position since I made the woman sit on the floor. Every time one of his punches drew blood or mad he woman scream, he looked back at me for to make sure I saw it. After a while I decided to show him how to throw a knee. I demonstrated the motions but didn't make contact because I wanted to keep her conscious. Without her yelps and cries, Zach wouldn't have been able to tell how affective a hit was. It was kind of like his scoring system. He did the knee as I showed him but I hand to explain that he should hold onto the hair and pull toward his knee when he did it.

So, this went on for well over an hour. After I showed him some moves and he had a chance to practice them, I let him just go off on her. I told him to see if he was able to kill her without a weapon. He went total bat shit on that woman, throwing fists, knees, and elbows as fast as he could. The woman surprisingly became unconscious somewhere in the mini fists of fury demo. She was still alive though and Zach was starting to get discouraged. I told him it just requires practice and to never give up. He turned back with his second wind and kept kicking as hard as he could. He felt the pulse again and it was still there. Zach let out a crazy sounding roar and grabbed the hammer that was laying on the edge of the table. He started hitting the woman in the top and side of the head until she had no more energy. He then dropped to his knees and reached over to check the pulse again. He held up the hammer and said yay.

He then walked back into the front room without making eye contact and turned on the tv. I looked back at the body. I could hardly recognize it was human. He turned it into a pile of hamburger with scattered skull fragments. At that moment, I realized that he either had a good since of humor or no common sense. I mean, why would he even check for a pulse after that? I decided to lighten the mood. I carefully removed one of the breasts from the woman's body. It is a lot harder than it sounds. I had to find a very sharp knife and once the skin was removed, the contents wanted to slide out. It took a bit of time but I finally got it off completely and in one piece. I sat down beside Zach and placed it on this lap and told him not to be a boob. That was the best laugh I've heard in a long time. He gets my jokes. I don't think many other people would have found it that funny.

October 11, 2014 (1:00 a.m.)   Warrenton, VA

Dear Diary, we woke up yesterday morning around 6am and decided it was time to leave. The house was starting to get that old body smell and we were both getting board. We're obviously not meant to be homebodies. No one was missing the family so we took their car and just started heading north, taking all back roads and city strips. The ride shouldn't have taken as long as it did but I want to stay off main roads since I know they're having traffic stops. We didn't really have a plan on where we would end up. We were just driving. We stopped here because we saw a sign for a haunted corn maze and decided to take advantage of it.

We stopped by a store to pick up a couple Halloween costumes for the event and put them into a book bag. It felt pretty cool walking around in a store. I have avoided them for a while. No one looks at us as different. We look like a normal family with normal Halloween plans. We made it to the maze while it was still daylight so we just drove around residential streets looking for a place to spend the night if we needed to. When the sun was down, we went back and parked in the grass parking lot. It was a full house. All we had equipped was a knife each and our costumes in the book bag. I had Zach wear the bag so it would be less suspicious. Once we made it through the line, we broke clear of our group by walking slowly. Once no one was in sight we ran off trail into the corn.

There, we got into our costumes. The plan was to appear to be employees. He has a bloody doctor's outfit and I had a Jason mask. Unfortunately, they didn't have the jumpsuit but it worked out anyway. We took out our knives and went to the edge of the trail. When a group of people walked by, we would jump at them, making them jump. They laughed and kept walking. Everyone believed they would be safe in the corn maze because it is against the rules to actually hurt someone. However, once you have made it past all of those beliefs and restrictions, no one is really safe. There was a guy that was walking alone, which made it pretty easy. When he saw us, he just snickered and walked on. He had bushy black hair, a black shirt, and some neck tattoos. I guess he was going after the inmate look.

Well, I grabbed his throat and took him down backwards. I stuck him in the side of the throat with a knife while Zach jumped on his belly and started with his signature rapid slasher routine. Just then, another group of people walked beside us. I paused because there were like five of them and I didn't know what to do. Zach just kept stabbing. One girl let out a scream but it was followed by a laugh. They all just kept walking. I overheard one teenager grumble, "Looks so fake." We dragged the body out of sight into the corn and went back to our posts.

I heard a guy with a chainsaw a couple yards down the trail getting a lot of attention. We walked the corn beside the trail until we reached his back. He was alone, doing his own thing. We watched him for a bit. He was very fat, dressed up in a bloody farmers outfit, and wielding a bladeless chainsaw. When there was no sign of a group, I walked up through the corn and jumped out, ramming the knife into the back of his neck. Zach stood back while I did because he wasn't convinced the chainsaw wasn't dangerous. The guy put up a little struggle but he didn't last long. Another group of people walked by as I removed my knife from his side. Yeah, I had ahold of it when he lunged away from me and I had to reinsert it into his lung.

Anyway, the group stopped to watch, thinking it was part of the act. When they walked on, I thought about dragging the body into the corn but decided against it since everyone thought it was fake anyway. Zach and I walked back through the corn and found another part of the trail. Here, was a teenage couple holding hands while the girl exaggerated her fear in an effort to seek more attention from the boy. I stood with my back facing the corn as they approached us, while Zach, now even bloodier than before, stood in the middle of the path. The girl screamed but the boy ensured her it was just for show. She didn't even see me since her attention was on the creepy little doctor blocking their path.

The boy approached Zach in an attempt to show his girlfriend his bravery. What a fool though. Zach had stabbed him in the stomach about three times before the girl realized what was going on. He turned slowly and dropped to his knees, and then to the ground. The girl gave a loud scream but I quickly muffled it and pulled her into the corn. I gave my mask to Zach and told him to quickly put it on the body so he blends into the show. He did, but as soon as he started to walk back toward us, a girl about his age ran up on him and yelled for her dad to hurry up. She held her hands up to her mouth in response to the sight of Zach and the body. She screamed to her dad, "Hurry, you need to see this one!" She walked closer to Zach, attempting to overcome her initial fear.

Zach stuck the knife into her heart and dragged her into the woods to meet us. The girl I was holding down screamed when she saw what the doctor dragged in. I reached up and twisted off an ear of corn. I then put the tip in her mouth and used almost all of my strength and body weight to drive it a quarter of the way down her throat. I think she died before I made it that far but I had to make sure by slicing her jugular and letting her bleed out. The funny part is that I could feel my knife hitting the corncob when I did. The dad was very overweight, which may have explained his inability to keep up with his daughter. He was accompanied by a boy and another girl, all about the same age. I don't know why she was allowed to stray out of sight. As he walked by, he stepped over the Jason body and yelled, "Emily!" I could tell he was nervous but he wasn't about to move any faster. They kept walking, assuming she was further in the maze.

We decided we had enough fun in the maze so we needed a place to spend the night. She removed her costume and put it back in the bag. I pulled the guy into the corn and reclaimed my mask. We walked the remainder of the trail and pretended to be startled whenever someone jumped out at us. At our pace, we passed the dad and the kids. He stopped us to ask if we saw a little girl. He then went into describing Emily. We told him we hadn't and continued the path. When we got out, we were back at the parking lot. It was sort of confusing since we were in there for so long and all we did was walk in a big circle. We went back to our car and gave each other a high five when we had our seat belts on. I haven't had that much fun for a while. I love the Halloween season.

We've just been sitting in a hotel parking lot for a while. It seems like the perfect place to look inconspicuous. Cars are expected to come and go at all hours and everyone is a stranger to each other.

Whenever someone walks by, I just start looking around in the car for something and they keep walking. I wish we could just go in and have another hotel night like we did back in the day but I am concerned with being identified. I recognize that no one has my face yet but if I'm on camera checking into a hotel with a bloody kid on the same night of the cornfield murders, I'm sure they'll put one and two together. That's when they would have my ID. Hmm, maybe I should just drive all night and make it to the ocean. That would be a good place to relax for a while.

October 11, 2014 (7:00 a.m.)
Virginia Beach, VA

Dear Diary, what the fuck? I just drove all morning, one side road after another to have a relaxing day on the beach. But what do I get? Cold windy-ass rain! We're in another hotel parking lot and now I don't know what to do next. I wonder if there's anything else fun to do around here that is inside. I'm hungry and I bet Zach is too. I'm trying to get off eating people for a while though. I haven't felt that well ever since my last meal of mom and gravy. Zach seems fine but I really don't want to take any chances. I remember hearing something several years ago about how people can die from eating other people. I think it's better to resist and live. Well, we're going to find somewhere to eat and hopefully something to do. I should have known better than to try to do the beach in October. I feel like I'm losing my mind more and more every day. Talk to you later Diary.

October 11, 2014 (9:00 p.m.)   Charleston, WV

Dear Diary, I have decided to go back to Erica and try to live a normal life. Zach and I had to buy souvenir hoody sweaters and umbrellas from the beach so we could walk around. We walked the beach, finding shell fragments and putting them in our book bag. He was excited every time he found one. I had to cut him off after a while though since we were running out of room. I talked to him about Erica and Evan. He appears to be fine with the idea of having a house, mom, and little brother. We also discussed the fact that we would have to stop our murder journey and stop eating people. He agreed to live that life but he wanted to have one more go before turning normal as he put it. I agreed but reinforced why living the normal life is better. I told him that we would always have food and no one would be hunting for us. I told him that he wouldn't be able to go to school but we would teach him everything he needs to learn at home. Just talking about it brought goose bumps to my skin. I remembered how it felt when that was my plan in the beginning.

We ended up in Charleston because it seems to be about half way and a good place to pull off our last mission. I told him that he could lead on this one and I'd help him. I wanted him to have the full experience before we check out. He was up on his knees in the passenger seat as we drove around. He talked more today than he has since Abram. Once, he told me to pull into a driveway so he could check it out. He looked around and noticed a camera on the neighbor's house aiming at the road and decided against it. I was proud of him for that observation.

We then passed a church with a couple cars. He wanted to stop there. I thought it was strange that people were in church on a Saturday but who am I to judge. I pulled in and asked him for his plan. He looked around and looked back at me. He said, "People in church want to die don't they?" I thought about it for a second and agreed. That's all they talk about all day. They just want to meet their creator. Perhaps we could have our last experience and perform a good deed all at the same time. I forgot to mention that between walking in the rain to get an umbrella and changing in the car, we were no longer looking suspicious.

We walked into the front door and there was an old man in a suit standing in the entryway. He asked us if we were there to confess. I told him we were just passing by and we felt like God wanted us to be there. I told him that we had no idea what was going on or why people were there on a Saturday. He was excited about God telling us to come there. He explained that it was open confession for another 30 minutes and anyone is welcome to enter. He pointed us toward a room with a confession booth and I told him thanks. While walking down the hall, I stepped aside and told Zach that it was his show. I had the gun under my shirt just in case anything got crazy. All he had was a knife to work with.

He walked into the confession room and sat at one of the benches. I followed his lead, anxious to see what he would do. There were about 4 other people there besides us. He did nothing but sit there. I was beginning to wonder if he was actually planning to go to confession and move on. He kept looking at the clock. It turned out, he was waiting for everyone else to leave. When the last old couple walked out of the confession room, the guy from the door came in and said the front door was locked but we were welcome to take all the time we need before entering the booth. I told him thanks and looked at Zach and asked what the plan was. He said, "There are only 2 people in a locked building." He asked me to take out the doorman while he spoke with the preacher.

He then got up and walked into the booth. I looked back and the old man was sitting in a bench toward the back of the room smiling ear to ear while he read the bible. He was obviously very happy about his promise of an afterlife. I wanted to grant him this gift early without pain since he was so nice to us earlier. I walked past him and told him I'd be waiting out front. After he turned back to his reading, I tiptoed up behind him and sliced the front of his throat so hard it felt like I almost touched the spinal bones. I then walked up to the booth and listened in to the conversation. Zach was opening up to him and talking about the rapes he experienced by Abram and his friend. He told the preacher it was his uncle to keep suspicions down. I was saddened by the story but was a bit uncomfortable with the preacher's responses. Instead of providing support and asking how it all stopped, he was just asking for more details about the attacks.

He said it was perfectly normal to have that kind of relationship with a man but the world just doesn't want to face it. He said his uncle was a bad man for being so mean about it and explained that if he did it with love, he could have been very happy. I swung open the preacher's door in anger and he was masturbating while looking in through a hole at Zach. I drop kicked him in the face and pulled him out of the stall by his feet. Zach ran out laughing. He said, "Fuck you dirty old bastard!" Somehow, he must have known what the preacher was doing or at least how he was. He was curled up into a ball, begging me to not hurt him. He said it wasn't what it looked like. He said he had a condition that he couldn't help. He said he'd never hurt him. I let him stay on the ground and asked Zach what he wanted to do to him.

At this point, Zach had decided it was time to confess for real. He asked me to tie him up somehow. I found some thick blue ribbon around the altar and used it to restrain him to a statue of Jesus. I sat on the front bench while Zach stood there and told him who we were and some of the things we had done. He then told him that he was definitely going to die tonight. The man started crying and praying. He asked us to spare him but I responded with, "Seriously?"

I pointed to the door guy, which made the preacher scream and put his head down in prayer even longer. I was curious to see what Zach had planned because it had been a while since we were in this position. I'm starting to remember more as we go. Zach sat down beside me and asked me how being saved works. I told him that you ask for Jesus to come into your heart and he washes away your sin. He asked if he would forgive anyone for anything. I told him I'm pretty sure that's how it works. He asked if there's any way to make sure someone goes to hell. I then knew what he was planning, which was genius. I told him to deny God is a ticket to hell from what I have been told. He then asked for my gun.

I gave it to him but told him not to use it until I came back. I walked out the front door and looked around the building to confirm we were fairly distant from neighboring houses. Luckily, the closest one had all of the lights off. If they would wake from the noise, they might not know what it was. I walked back in, locked the door, and told him it was all clear. That he can't fire more than one shot since sleeping neighbors are close. He walked over to the preacher and told them that we have let some people go and that not all we have captured have been killed. He said that all they had to do is deny God and promise not to tell anyone. The preacher refused at first. Zach pointed the gun at him and he almost said the words but dropped down and refused again.

Zach took out his knife and went behind the statue. He told the guy to do it or die painfully. He slowly shoved the knife into his kidney area. The guy screamed in pain, denying God and promising not to tell anyone. I was amazed at how easy he was willing to give up everlasting peace just to have a couple more years on this shit ball of a planet. Zach quickly shot the guy in the back of the head before he had a chance to take it back or ask for forgiveness. He ran toward the front door shouting for me to follow. I didn't know what the rush was until we got into the car. Zach said that the preacher's cell phone rang while I was outside. He said that with no answer, someone is probably going to be looking for him.

I was so proud of his level of wisdom maturity in all of this. It was almost spooky. As we drove off, I couldn't help but to think that this one may have been the worst kill yet, religiously speaking. I have always been focused primarily on ending someone's life on this earth and nothing else. If they pray, I let them pray. I don't think about what happens next. Not Zach; he took an old man that had been playing the system his whole life and turned the tables on him. I bet he was living his perverted life in the darkness and praying every time he did something sinful so he could still get to heaven. He was probably one of those people that thought he could live every day the way he wants and ask for forgiveness right at the finish line. I guarantee he was planning to ask for forgiveness if we let him live. But now, he's definitely burning in hell, or perhaps just dead like a fly. I don't know anymore. The last thing he ever did with his dedicated preacher life was to deny God. Freak'n Priceless. We're in a fast food parking lot so I can get my thoughts on paper before they disappear. This is all for now though because the drive through lady has looked over at us more than once. Next stop, my Erica.

October 12, 2014 (7:20 p.m.)   Frankfort, KY

Dear Diary, Erica was so excited to see me. When we pulled in, I began getting nervous. Zach, on the other hand, looked a little depressed. I asked him if everything was okay and he said he just wanted to eat someone. I told him I felt the same way but this is the only way we could truly be a family. I gave him a big hug, and then we walked to the door. Erica got instant tears in her eyes as she quickly wrapped her arms around me. She stepped back and asked if it was Heather beside me. I told her yes but we prefer Zach and that he would be her new son. She went down and gave him a big hug, welcoming him to the family.

I could tell that Zach was a little uncomfortable with all of the attention. Erica rushed us in to show Zach his new brother. The girl in him instantly came out as he started playing with his brother's finger. I asked if he would be ok watching him while we went in the room to take a nap. Zach agreed, and I followed Erica to the bedroom, where we quietly made love and held each other tightly. She told me that the Zach's kidnapping from the children's home had made worldwide news. In fact, everything I have done has put me at number one on the America's Most Wanted. She said it seems like everyone with a pulse is on a manhunt for me but no one knows who I am. All they have is a warehouse full of random evidence and a child's description. She said this is the perfect time to settle down and throw in the towel. I completely agree with her because now that I have her and Zach in the same house, there's nothing more I could desire.

When we walked back out, Zach and Evan were both asleep in the recliner. It was a picture perfect moment. He must have been very exhausted to just pass out like that. Erica took me out back to show me our new dog. It was a brown boxer with a white circle of fur on his back. His name is Spot – I teased her about the lack of originality. Today, we all went grocery shopping as a family for the first time. We walked around checking the price on food and looking at the nutrition facts just like everyone else. We were walking among the living and Zach squeezed my hand the whole time. He pointed out that a boy walked into the restroom by himself. I had to bend down and whisper to Zach that we cannot do anything in this town or they'll know we're here. We need to stop and live normal. I told him to just watch all of the other kids and see how they act so he can blend in. I think this is going to be a difficult adjustment for him.

October 13, 2014 (7:30 p.m.)
Frankfort, KY (Home)

Dear Diary, today we started decorating the house for Halloween and bought trick or treat costumes for the kid. We had to throw away his doctor one. Zach will be a zombie and Evan will be a little lion. I thought Zach would be enjoying all of this quality family time but he just seemed to be getting more distant. But last night, I realized I still had a dead family's car so I had to go dump it a couple hours north. Zach went with me and all he could talk about was getting back on the road. It was a long awkward drive as I talked to him about what would happen to me if we were caught. I told him that at the moment, we can be in each other's life forever but if we continue, and we get caught, they would kill me. He laid his head on my lap and sighed sadly.

We drove to a dump, where we were just going to let them have it for scrap but then I had a better idea that Zach jumped all over. I figured we could take this opportunity to throw the cops on a false trail. We have been heading north, killing along the way. If we killed some a couple hours north of home, the investigation would pass us up. We drove around until we saw a woman out night jogging. I told Zach the plan and drove about forty yards past the woman to let him out. It was dark enough that I felt confident she didn't see us. He sat on the curb and pretended to cry as I drove up and around the corner. I got out stood by the open trunk and waited for him to bring her into the trap.

He waited for the woman to approach him. He told her that he left his bedroom window to walk around but was scared to walk back home alone. Obviously the woman offered to help. When they got around the corner, I acted like a concerned dad. I said, "There you are Tommy! What are you doing out here?!" Zach put his head down and got into the passenger side. I thanked the woman with a handshake and as soon as she turned away from me, I hit her in the back of the head with the car's tire iron. I then shoved her in the trunk and took off down the street.

While I looked for a dumpsite, Zach climbed in the back seat and pulled down the backrest to reveal the trunk. He reached in and pulled out her hand, tugging until her whole arm was through the hole. I watched this in the rear view but when he pulled out his knife and started carving off meat, I reminded him we were going to give that up. He said, "One last time. Please." I couldn't say no to those puppy dog eyes, plus I was thinking the same thing. I told him to just get one arm and put it in a plastic bag that was trashing up the floorboard. We would take some to go. He smiled and did a I asked.

We left the car in the driveway of a house that was for sale and knocked over the for sale sign. We then kept walking until we reached a payphone by a gas station and called a cab. We had him drop us off several blocks from our house just for safe measure. So here we are. Zach is chipper and really getting into the holiday spirit. I love watching my boys play together. I can't wait until Evan can talk in full sentences. For dinner, I made a special meal for Zach and myself. Erica was fine with having a separate dish because I told her the meat we had in the fridge was rabbit. I knew she thought they were too cute to eat. She didn't like the idea of it but didn't try to push her beliefs on us. We both ate so much we felt like we were going to pop but there were no leftovers. We both knew that would be the last time we had a meal like that, so we made it count.

October 14, 2014 (5:00 p.m.)   Home

Dear Diary, today we just stayed around the house all day. The three of us that could read, played board games and read books. Erica had a whole bookshelf of children's books that she had purchased at a library sale. Zach is very rusty on his reading but he is picking back up on it. I'm loving my life. I just wish he would be more engaged in our family activities.

October 15, 2014 (7:00 p.m.)   Home

Dear Diary, I woke up to a scream from Erica. I ran out back, where it came from and she was sitting there slumped over the dog. All of the skin had been removed and the leash was wrapped around its neck, appearing to be the cause of death. Erica didn't know who did it but I did. I walked in the house and asked Zach, who was eating cereal in front of the TV. He admitted it to me and said that he felt like he needed to kill something and couldn't help it. I told him that it was fine but to not tell his mom.

He helped me dig the hold to bury the dog after he was done eating. I could feel the tension in the air because in the back of my head, I think Erica believed I was responsible. I went into the bathroom and there was the wizard cat sitting on the toilet taking a shit. He was grunting loudly. I asked him to keep it down and why he had come back. He told me I'm not being a good father. He said that there's no reason to be here. I told him that we were a happy family now and that isn't going to change. He started to say something else but I just cupped my ears like a spoiled child and kept saying, "na na na na." When I removed my hands and opened my eyes, he was gone. I looked in the toilet, which still contained his oversize kitty turds. I really don't care what he says anymore. I know he's just in my head.

I feel that Zach is resisting this lifestyle or at least that he doesn't feel comfortable in it. He spends a lot of time standing by the front screen door just staring out into the street. I have learned to not ask him what he's thinking because it's always, "Nothing." It bothers me that he is becoming more distant but I still think it is for the best that we stay here. One day he will forget all about what we have been through and live a normal life. Perhaps one day he will thank me for bringing him here. I can't really get him to eat that much real food. He says he misses the meat. Earlier today I walked in on him cutting his knee with a piece of glass he found on the side of the house. I just walked away to give him his alone time.

October 16, 2014 (6:00 p.m.)   Home

Dear Diary, Zach came in and slept in our bed last night. He was very sweaty and a little tense. I asked him what was wrong and he just said, "Nothing." I was concerned that he was starting to feel neglected because, until now, it was just me and him. I can see how having an instant family might make him feel a little left out. I told him that we would do something together in the morning, just the two of us. He rolled over, gave me a hug, and went to sleep.

Well, this morning I had to live up to my promise but I didn't know what to do. I talked to Erica and told her that I was going to take him out alone for a while. She gave me her keys and her only words were, "Please don't do anything stupid." I took him to a park and let him play but he wasn't that interested. He only sat on the bench beside me. I asked him if there was anything he would like to do. He said that he would really like to hurt someone. He told me that he can't get confortable unless he sees someone die. I never really noticed how empty his eyes are. I used to stare into them and see so much life and love. I almost feel like I'm talking to a robot or an empty body of some sort. I am very saddened by the thought of Zach fading away. I told him to try to resist and it will all pay off.

I tried to change the subject to Trick or Treat but it fell on deaf ears. He just shrugged his shoulders as he stared at the park patrons like a bucket of chicken wings. For me, I do feel a pull toward feeling the blood, seeing the shimmer, and tasting the body. However, I have all three of my loves in one house, so it is easy for me to distract myself. I will have Erica as my wife and adopt Evan legit. When we came home, Zach just went to the back yard and sat by the dog burial for a while before returning to eat a hotdog and go to bed. I'll give him his space for now. The more he is around his new mom and brother, the more he will learn to accept them and that this is the life for him.

October 17, 2014 (5:35 p.m.)   Home

Dear Diary, I'm starting to get my head together. I don't know how long I've been lost but I'm just glad to be here. Today, I spent most of my day with Evan and Erica at the Pediatrician's for his well-child appointment. He is recognizing me as his dad more and more each day. It feels amazing when he squeezes my finger and stares into my eyes with a big smile. The doctor even handed him to me for the shots, referring to me as the dad. That felt awesome. His eyes are so full of life and joy. Just holding him makes me forget my worries. I can tell how much Erica loves it that we have that bond. She just watches us and smiles.

Zach wanted to stay home to watch some cartoons. I know he's technically too young to stay home alone but he is not an average kid. He is much more mature and responsible than he is expected to be. Even though I have a spot in my heart for Evan, no one can compare to my Zach. I'm so proud of him for sticking in there to make this change. I know it is a lot for him but it will be better in the long run for sure. When we came home, he was in the yard, talking to a neighbor boy who looked a little younger than him. During dinner, he told me all about the boy and that he might come over to play some day. This made me feel amazing because I could see Zach starting to come around. I loved seeing his smile. I want to capture that moment in my mind forever. All of us sitting around the table, Evan at his high chair, and everyone smiling at the same time. Priceless.

October 18, 2014 (9:00 p.m.)   Home

Dear Diary, I don't know what to do with Zach. I am starting to doubt his ability to change but I have to keep trying. Again, we all left the house but he wanted to stay home alone. After we did our errands and picked up some fast food, we came home. Zach came straight to me like an eager puppy. He gave me a hug and told me how much better he is feeling today. He apologized for being grumpy lately. Erica was excited by this news as well and went to give Zach a big hug.

While we were eating lunch, the neighbor came over and asked if Blake was still over here. I told him I haven't seen him today and the man told me that his son told him he was coming to play with Zach. I asked Zach to come to the door and reply to the man. Zach said he hadn't seen him and went back to the kitchen. After lunch, I pulled Zach aside and asked where the boy was. He led me out back to the sand box and started moving some sand with his hand. Less than an inch under the sand, the boy's face was revealed. He smiled as big as his lips would allow and said, "I did it with my bare hands." I got angry and told them that this is our house and we cannot have this kind of attention.

I didn't even want him to explain how he did it because I wasn't interested. I just knew we needed to get rid of the body. I buried the face again and went into the house to get an old sheet. Zach followed behind me. Luckily Erica was in the shower. After hearing the water, I ensured Evan was in his playpen and hurried back to the sand box. We both looked around and no one was to be seen so I gathered the body in the sheet and wrapped it up as quickly as I could. I didn't wrap it like on the movie or anything because I didn't want to be obvious. I balled him up in the middle and pulled all the corners in to appear as I was only carrying a bag of junk or something. We casually took it to the trunk and dropped it in. No one noticed. Zach was smart enough to grab a shovel as well.

After Erica's shower, I told her I was going to take Zach out again. We drove for a while until we came to a cemetery and a light bulb went off in my head. Why would someone need to dig a grave twice? We drove to the back where no one could see us from the road. I found an older looking grave and cut the sod in squares until the size was big enough. I grabbed the sheet from the trunk and left the body. I removed the sod and dug a hole, throwing all of the dirt onto the sheet. Once the hole was a couple feet deeper than the boy was thick, I tossed him in. We both threw the dirt back in until it was almost sod level.

At that point I was just going to throw the sod back on to even it out and run but I remembered that as the body decomposes, the dirt might sag. I mounded the dirt over the hole and slid a corner of the sheet over. I then ran over it a couple times with the car to make sure it was good and packed. There was still a bit of a mound so I just removed it back to the sheet and placed the sod. I wrapped the excess dirt and put it in the trunk. After a little poking and pulling, the grave looked untouched. Now give me a reason why anyone would look there.

I was so mad at Zach that I didn't even talk to him on the way home. I just couldn't understand why he would do something so stupid. It's like he doesn't care if we get caught or not. Everything I do, I do for him. If it wasn't for him, I wouldn't even be alive in the first place. All I wish is that he could change with me. When we came in the door, Zach went to his room and didn't eat dinner. I feel bad for leaving it that way but he needs to realize I'm upset with him. That's the only way he will change.

October 19, 2014 (8:10 a.m.)   Hell

Dear Diary, I'm dying. This is the last statement of life. My arms are numb and I can't breathe. There is no more! There is no more! WHY!? Zach, Why!" Zach… Oh Erica I'm sorry. My little Evan. I'm leaving this world right now. These will be my last words Diary. It has been a great journey but it is over. So over. I am trying to maintain long enough to get these events on paper but I can't steady my hand. I can't keep my eyes on the paper. I can't breathe.

I woke up this morning to a bang. It startled me so I sat up wondering what woke me up. Then I heard it again. It was in the house! It was my gun! Why, Zach, Why!? I can't breathe. My heart has stopped. I cannot feel my heart beat. My vision is fading. Please God give me strength to finish these words. Please God. I'm sorry for everything I have done. Please forgive me of my sins. I repent. I am done. I am dying. It is over. I ran into the kitchen, where Zach was standing there holding my gun smiling so proudly. Smiling and smiling. Pancakes were served and they were dead. Zach had shot Erica in the back of the head and then Evan between the eyes.

Diary, I couldn't think. Everything started to turn black just like it is now. Let me fight this off until these words are in stone. Let me finish my thoughts. I can't breathe. My heartbeat has stopped. I am dead. When I saw them, I yelled at Zach and Zach vanished. I thought it was a dream. I thought Zach just vanished. I suddenly realized I was standing about five feet closer to the table than I was before. I had moved. I knew what happened. I knew it. I ran around the house looking for Zach. I kept yelling that everything would be okay and that I'll get over it. I yelled that we can go on the road again. I made all the promises I wish I had made to him before this because I felt in my gut that something was wrong.

I came to the bathroom where Zach's head was in the sink and his body was in the tub. I killed my boy! He didn't ask for any of this. I brought him here. We could have continued living on the road for the rest of our lives. Now he is gone! He is gone! And I can't breathe. I'm sitting in the corner of the living room trying to silence the cat. He is standing on the back of the couch hissing at me. It is constant, steady, and ear shattering. He is pointing at me with his gross human finger. I asked him to stop but his hiss is not stopping. I officially can't walk now. I tried to get up but I can't walk. I don't have a heartbeat. I'm sorry, Zach. I have to close my eyes now. Something is pulling them shut. I'm sorry Zach!

October 19, 2014 (4:00 p.m.)   Living Room

Hello Diary, my name is Zach. I don't know where my dad is, but he left this book. I know he always writes in it and never leaves it any place. I am hoping he comes home soon because I want to show him what I did to the woman and boy who were keeping us apart. I want to show him it can just be me and him again now. I have been here for a while and I don't know where he is. Maybe he went to the store. I will watch some cartoons and wait for him because I know he will be so happy to see it is only me and him again. I hope he is not mad that I am writing in his book. He loves this book for some reason. I love him. When we go driving again I want to see if I can drive. If he doesn't come back for me, I might need to go without him because maybe he is in jail and I don't want to go to jail too.

Bye

About Your Author

J. Steffy lives a normal family life with normal job and a not so normal cat.

He has done work with the criminally insane, giving him the unique insight reflected in his writing.

He has an extremely short attention span, often causing him to lose interest while trying to read.

This inspired him to write, and to target an audience that craves nonstop action from cover to cover.

Other HellBound Books Titles
Available at: www.hellboundbookspublishing.com

The Children of Hydesville

"A contemporary ghost story made all the more terrifying for being based upon actual events."

When the terrifying entity that Maggie and Katie Fox unleashed in Hydesville in 1848 returns in 2018, a gallery owner, his wife, a journalist and her boyfriend join forces to battle it.

Manhattanites Derek David and his wife Edith receive an invitation to visit the Keilgarden Colony. Founded in 1948 with funds from Derek's great grandfather, the Colony is a secluded community dedicated to nurturing children with psychic abilities. Located five hours north of the city in the village of Hydesville, the compound was built on land that includes the cottage where Maggie and Katie Fox first heard the ghostly rappings in 1848 which started the Spiritualist movement.

The Southern House

There are some places that lie where the barrier between worlds is thin and growing thinner. These corridors are as old as the Earth itself, hidden in dark and forgotten places, waiting to be found. There is a being who stalks these places and travels between those worlds. He was given the name Mr. Shift by generations of children and madmen.

Just as Hickory Grimble hits rock bottom, he inherits his grandparents' farm and believes his luck is changing. He soon finds he inherited more than money and land.

Haunted by his own inner demons, now he has new problems. He begins to see strange creatures on the dark, sprawling acreage, animals that have no business living in middle Tennessee. He also discovers a decrepit, abandoned house in the forest that never seems to be in the same place twice.

Balanced on a razor's edge between, addiction and fate, Hick is now face to face with an ancient evil that has returned once more to claim more of the town's children.

Them

Ray Sanders returns home from Florida to bury his mother.

Soon, the supernatural evidence behind his mother's demise begins to surface in the form of dreams and mysterious happenings.

During all of the madness, Sanders must face his destiny and vanquish the generations-old evil that has plagued his family since the 1800's…

In 1854, Louis Sanders, with the help of Elias Atkins, dug a well to provide water to the family farm. What they did not anticipate was the water to be infested with Odomulites - ancient sins. These malevolent beings - were trapped in our world on their way to the spirit world - formed a pact of protection with both Sanders and Atkins; the families would serve as guardians of the Odomulite nests and in return, a blind eye would be cast when the Odomulites took host bodies to inhabit and feed upon. It was this pact, which in 2016 would propel Sanders and Julie Fontaine - a young woman with a special connection to the Spirit World - into the heart of the last active nest to rid the town of its insidious Odomulite population.

Blood in The Woods

Based upon true events...

For Jody, growing up in the late eighties and early nineties in the small Louisiana town of Hammond with his best friend Jack was filled with wonderful childhood memories.

Time spent playing in the woods, shooting pellet guns, blowing up mailboxes, fighting at school and upon the dawning of interest in the fairer sex, their carefree lives typical of children with few responsibilities and no worries beyond the next pop-quiz or getting to second base. As they grow older together and experience the joys and pains of life, love, family and friendship, they uncover a grim secret that their home town has kept, and through little more than an innocent, idle curiosity, Jody and Jack stumble upon something horrific in the woods and their lives quickly take a most sinister and dangerous turn as they find themselves hunted by an unspeakable evil...

No Rest For The Wicked

From beyond the grave, a murderous wife seeks to complete her revenge on those who betrayed her in life; a powerless domestic still fears for her immortal soul while trying to scare off anyone who comes too close; and the former plantation master - a sadistic doctor who puts more faith in the teachings of de Sade than the Bible - battle amongst themselves and with the living to reveal or keep hidden the dark secrets that prevent any of them from resting in peace. When Eric and Grace McLaughlin purchase Greenbrier Plantation, their dreams are just as big as those who have tried to tame the place before them. But, the doctor has learned a thing or two over his many years in the afterlife, is putting those new skills to the test, and will go to great lengths in order to gain the upper hand. While Grace digs into the death-filled history of her new home, Eric soon becomes a pawn of the doctor's unsavory desires and rapidly growing power, and is hell-bent on stopping her.

"If you're looking for a chilling ghost story filled with mystery and escalating tension, look no further. No Rest for the Wicked is the real deal - an expansive, unfolding riddle between the living and the dead."
Hunter Shea - author of *"Tortures of the Damned"* & *"We Are Always Watching"*

Worship Me

Something is listening to the prayers of St. Paul's United Church, but it's not the god they asked for; it's something much, much older.

A quiet Sunday service turns into a living hell when this ancient entity descends upon the house of worship and claims the congregation for its own.

The terrified churchgoers must now prove their loyalty to their new god by giving it one of their children or in two days time it will return and destroy them all.

As fear rips the congregation apart, it becomes clear that if they're to survive this untold horror, the faithful must become the faithless and enter into a battle against God itself.

But as time runs out, they discover that true monsters come not from heaven or hell…
…they come from within.

Demons, Devils and Denizens of Hell: Vol, 2

The second volume in HellBound Books' outstanding horror anthology fair teems with tales of Hades' finest citizens – both resident and vacationing in our earthly realm…

Compiled by the inimitable P. Mattern and featuring: Savannah Morgan, Andrew MacKay, Jaap Boekestein, James H Longmore, Stephanie Kelley, Ryan Woods, James Nichols, P. Mattern, Marcus Mattern, Gerri R Gray, and legion more…

Shopping List 2: Another Horror Anthology

Once again, HellBound Books brings you an outstanding collection of horror, dark, slippery things, and supernatural terror - all from the very best up and coming minds in the genre.

We have given each and every one of our authors the opportunity to have their shopping lists read by you, the most wonderful reading public, and have the darkest corners of their creative psyche laid bare for all to see...

In all, 21 stories to chill the soul, tingle the spine and keep you awake in the cold, murky hours of the night from: Erin Lee, The Truth Artist, John Barackman, Serena Daniels, M.R. Wallace, Isobel Blackthorn, Alex Laybourne, Jason J. Nugent, Josh Darling, Jovan Jones, Nick Swain, Douglas Ford, Craig Bullock, Craig Bullock, Jeff C. Stevenson, PC3, David F Gray, Sergio Palumbo, Donna Maria McCarthy, David Clark & Megan E. Morales

**A HellBound Books LLC
Publication**

http://www.hellboundbookspublishing.com

Printed in the United States of America

www.ingramcontent.com/pod-product-compliance
Lightning Source LLC
Chambersburg PA
CBHW060544190726
48283CB00003B/857